A Fisherman's View

Available on Amazon.com

Screenplay version available

WeScreenplay Feedback - Hollywood's #1 Script
Coverage: RECOMMEND

*"Characters are so overwhelmingly complex and
powerful."*

*"One of the things that works brilliantly in this character
drama are the way in which thematic elements that are
introduced early tie back into the end of the narrative in
fascinating and revelatory ways."*

*"Dysfunctional family dramedies are an oft-seen genre, but
this one stands out."*

*"The family is full of uncomfortable behavior and good
intentions, which makes them fun to watch. We honestly
care about them as well, and their individual conflicts
never feel trite."*

To Lindsey, Tim, and Katie who always help me find beauty,
love, and courage.

And to Michele who reminds us to look for it every day.

An old bridge connecting a downtown with an uptown, allowing an assimilation of souls, their comings and goings, to melt and meld together and carry on with the daily necessities, all little seeds of love and caring, all striving for family.

Roberta Lee Gerber

A FISHERMAN'S VIEW

The first hint of light peers over Brooklyn, New York. Nestled at the foot of the Verrazano Bridge is Bay Ridge, a tight knit Irish neighborhood of retired cops and firefighters. It's a tiny two square mile community where everybody knows your business. Theresa Fitzgerald, thick, tough, 36 quickly going on 50, still in her Brooklyn Hospital nursing scrubs from the night shift, sits in her car staring at a red traffic light growing angrier with each passing second. "Come on. Come on."

She looks to the opposing green traffic signal. There's not another car in sight.

"This is ridiculous. Come on!"

The light glows red, and so does Theresa. She thinks for a moment, then exhales a puff of wind towards the light, as if she's blowing out the candles on a birthday cake. Tired of waiting, she hits the gas and runs the light. For an emergency room nurse in charge of patients, Theresa is not a very patient person.

Her worn Chevy Malibu drives past homes dotted along the street with green, white and orange Irish flags proudly draped alongside the American stars and stripes.

Years ago, the area was predominantly Italian, made famous in the 1970s by the sidewalk strutting of John Travolta in Saturday Night Fever. While the twenty-something professionals have taken over Williamsburg and Bushwick, hoping to make it the next Manhattan, the Irish carved out their own community inside Bay Ridge, an emerald oasis amidst the clutter and chaos of New York.

The driver's side door creeks open as Theresa gets out of the Chevy and climbs the steps of the 89th Street house she grew up in. It's old enough to be crappy, but not old enough to be charming. She approaches the door to find a man curled up asleep on her front porch. She gives a nudge. Nothing. Another nudge, only harder. "Hey!"

Michaleen Fitzgerald (Mik-a'-leen) rolls over with an impish smile, blue eyes that could make anyone fall in love with him, and an irresistible Irish brogue as thick as Guinness foam.

"Mornin', darlin'"

"How long you been out here?" asks Theresa.

"I don't know. Figured yiz was at work, so I settled in," he says through a yawn.

Elderly neighbor Rosemary Flanagan walks by in a pale housecoat, stockings and slippers, with her dog Topper, short for 'Top O' the Mornin' - as if the neighborhood needed another reason to hate this shitty little dog and Mrs. Flanagan's nosey intrusions. Theresa gives a forced, fake greeting just as Topper readies himself to take a shit on the sidewalk out front.

"Good morning, Mrs. Flanagan. Could you not let your dog…?"

"Everything all right up there, Theresa?" She really doesn't care if everything's all right up there.

"All good. Thank you."

Mrs. Flanagans' face shows her disgust when she spots the visitor on the porch. "Well, if it isn't Little Michael himself." She doesn't say it so much as spit the words.

"Tis indeed," says Michaleen sitting up, a disheveled mess, and scrubs a hand over his gray stubble.

"Get run out of Florida, did ye?" she asks with a hint of glee.

"Ah feck off, Rose. You had your chance at me back when I lived here." His hand rubs along the back of his neck. "And take that prissy little rat with ye."

"Well, I never," huffs Mrs. Flanagan as she picks up Topper and storms off.

"See, that's her problem. She needs a good snog, is all." Michaleen remarks. "Can't believe that cranky old lesbian's still alive."

"She's not a lesbian, Dad."

"Never made a move at me. I bet she's right, never been lai…"

"Stop!" Theresa hushes him before Michaleen can finish. She looks around to see if any other neighbors are watching.

"Come off the porch, will you?"

Michaleen gets to his feet and begins to pat himself down, touching his back pocket, front pocket, then lips. Theresa watches the strange ritual with a face full of confusion and her ever present impatience. All set, Mick grabs his backpack and shuffles inside.

****

The house was built in 1923, and other than some minor renovations done in the 70s and an occasional coat of paint, it's been the same physical structure and appearance since the day they moved in, particularly the kitchen with its worn linoleum floor, wood cabinetry, and off-white/yellowing appliances. No granite or stainless steel for the Fitzgeralds; their mother Bridget would never spend money so foolishly. *Everything works just fine, thank you very much. Besides, all the new products* (anything produced post 1979) are *probably made overseas* (the Orientals).

Michaleen takes a seat at the worn Formica table in the middle of the room, the same one his three kids squeezed around and elbowed each other relentlessly as teenagers. Theresa grabs her coffee the old-fashioned way, in a percolator, and throws bread into the toaster. No Keurig or hi-protein energy bar for her. She's old school, like everything else in this aged house, and toast with jam does just fine. Coffee first, always, and then she can face her father and listen to his reasons for being there.

The sound of slamming cups and cabinet doors only serves to emphasize the tension of the room.

"Aren't ye happy to see me?" asks Michaleen. "Ya seem a bit, I don't know, what's the word…agitated."

Theresa thinks on that for a second. Agitated. What a pussy word. She hates it. In her experience, you're either pissed off or about to become pissed off.

"Long shift. And I sat at that stupid light on Colonial for like an hour. Nobody on the road this time of day, but I gotta sit there and wait."

"It's green goin' the other way," he says. "Maybe ye need to change yer route. Or yer view."

She rolls her eyes. "No boat stories. It's too early."

"Everything changes eventually, darlin'. Red to green, green to yellow."

She joins him at the table with two cups of coffee and the almost burnt toast. "This the reason you drove all the way from Florida? To lecture me on traffic signals?" she asks, not sure she really wants to know the answer.

"Awe, it's a straight shot up 95, tha'. Turn right at the bridge. Besides, the girlfriend was drivin' me mad."

"Which one?" asks Theresa. "I lost count."

"The Italian bird, Maria. Or was it Margo. I can't remember. They're always callin'. Sex, sex, sex. It's relentless, I tell ya. Too controllin'. Just like yer mother."

"Yeah, well, we all know how that turned out," says Theresa as she spreads jam onto the toast.

"Me and yer mother had an amicable partin'."

"You're still technically married, you know," glares his daughter.

Michaleen gives a wave of his hand and states his case with a mouthful of toast.

"Insignificant details to be worked out between your mother and the Church. Her ways, not mine. I did all that nonsense when I was young. Stand up. Sit down. Kneel. Jaysus, them Catholics can't make up their mind. My money is still on God, it's just the institution I got no faith in. Too many diddlers and donations."

Theresa sips her morning coffee, surveying the situation. "Seems to me you've lost faith in a whole lot of institutions. Churches. Banks. Marriage."

These two were always good at verbal sparring, and Theresa just landed a hard one.

Michaleen was raised Catholic and was all in for a while. He's just not very good with rules. Although, he was proud to say, he'd never broken all the Ten Commandments - only about eight of them. It's not something he's particularly proud of, it's just a fact. He never killed anyone (Commandment 6) and he had great affection for his mother and father (Commandment 5), it was all the others that he had trouble with; Idols, Gods, swearin' and the like (that's 1,2,

3 right off the bat) The going to Mass every Sunday proved problematic after Saturday nights at Kelly's Tavern (Commandment 4), and he was especially challenged with any of the married ones (Commandments 7 and 10).

"And what's with the no meat?" he implores. "If it were up to your mother, she'd have me sittin' in Hell next to Hitler himself." He leans, as if he's talking to someone beside him. "Whatcha in for? Killing six million Jews. You? Cheeseburger on a Friday. Ooh, tough one, tha'."

Theresa just rolls her eyes. She's heard all this before.

"Hand me me Go bag, will ye darlin'?"

She strains to lift his backpack. "Jesus, what'd you pack in this thing? Not like you to stick around anywhere too long."

"Got things need tendin' to. By the way, she's dead."

"Maria's dead?"

"No."

"Margo?"

"No, no. Your mother. She passed a week ago." He delivers the news with a mouthful of food, as nonchalant and emotionless as reporting the Mets game ended in a tie. He plops a tin can on the table.

"Say hello, Bridget. It's Theresa. Your favorite daughter." His sarcasm is thick, and not lost on Theresa.

"What? Our mother died, and you didn't think to tell us?!"

"I'm telling you now, ain't I?" He reaches for a second piece of toast. She smacks his hand.

"I can't believe this. And you had her cremated?! She's Catholic."

"Aye, Catholic and claustrophobic - a tough combination, tha'. Ooh, she hated the box."

"It's called a coffin, Dad. So, you decide to put her in a coffee tin?"

"It's a nice, sturdy jar. Reminds me. She left instructions."

Of course Bridget left instructions. Even dead, she's still giving orders. Theresa sits, trying to wrap her head around it all. Michaleen reaches into his Go bag, dons black rimmed reading glasses and opens a note, handwritten in cursive, flowing penmanship.

"Let's see now. *'Water the plants. Clothes to St Vincent.'* Ah, here it is... *"and I want a proper service at Stanton's...not DeVito's, that Italian will charge too much."*

He glances up at Theresa. They both nod, as if to say, she's right.

"...and I'm to be cremated. No need to be givin' more money to the funeral home than necessary. I want the children there to represent the family. Richard should escort Fiona. I don't need those Shanty sisters of mine talking. And make sure Theresa gets there on time - she's always late, that one."

Theresa mutters to herself, "Jesus. Even from the grave." This had always been a part of the rhythm of their relationship. Theresa acted, Bridget commented. Jab. Jab. Hit.

Michaleen removes the glasses and looks at his daughter. He knows his wife was tough on the kids, especially Theresa.

"Now, I know losin' a parent can cut ye loose from your moorings, but ye need to..."

Theresa pulls away, too stubborn to be parented and too tough to be emotional.

"I'm fine. And I said no boat stories."

This is Michaleen's cue to head upstairs.

"Well, better call yer brother and sister. They'll need to be here."

He stands and performs the ritual - back pocket, front pocket, lips. Check.

"What...what the hell is all that?"

"Wallet. Keys. Teeth. I like to make sure I got 'em."

A wink, and he's gone. Theresa shakes her head, and stares at the tin jar that holds her mother's ashes.

MANHATTAN

Loud music fills a room of runway models in various states of dress. Through the doorway comes Richard Fitzgerald, 32, Manhattan's rising star of the design world. He's impeccably dressed in a tailored two-piece suit, white shirt, high collar, top three buttons undone revealing his neatly groomed chest, and the perfect amount of three-day stubble across his face. He commands the room, barking orders, reviewing the clothes on the models and constantly checking his watch.

"We are running six minutes behind, people. Let's go." He scans an outfit with disgust.

"No. No. This should drape the shoulder. This is too loose. Cut that."

His assistant, Tilton Masters, 26, rushes over. Skinny jeans. Plaid sport coat over a tight shirt. Man-scarf. He's trying way too hard. He always does.

"Richard? Excuse me. There's a call for you," he says with an unearned air of importance.

"What is this?"

"Um, a cell phone?" Tilton is a nervous wreck any time he's around Richard.

"I'm talking about the jacket."

Tilton goes from nervous to terrified.

"Scarf too much?" he asks.

"Way. And one button, Tilton. Always one button. It slims the silhouette."

"Yes, of course. Thank you, Richard."

Tilton undoes a button to remedy the situation. Richard is never wrong.   He waves off the cell phone and begins to work on the model's outfit.

"I can't talk now," he barks.

"She said it was important. It's um…it's your sister." Tilton says this with a tinge of hurt. He didn't know Richard had a sister. Or even a family.

Richard thinks before committing. "Which one?"

"Excuse me," asks Tilton into the cell phone, "Richard would like to know, which one."

He puts the phone to his chest, muffling the response.

"She said, the nice one."

Richard scans the model's outfit one last time, gives a "this will do" look, then takes the phone.

"Hey, Fi." Silence, then a look of concern. "Ok. Gimme 20 minutes."

He tosses the phone back to Tilton.

"Get my car keys."

"But, we have a show. What do I tell these people?"

Richard shoots him a look, one that says I don't care. Tilton takes that as his signal to go. Now.

"I'll get your keys."

****

Richard's office is sleek and modern with frosted glass for privacy, and transparent glass for views of busy Manhattan below him. Designer magazines are strewn across the floor. Photos adorn the walls; Richard with celebrity chefs, famous actors, models, sports figures. Tilton rushes in to find the keys.

He's in awe every time he enters this end of the building, and stops to take it all in. God, he wants this office, this life, so much. He looks around suspiciously, then slides Richard's desk drawer open. A huge designer sketch pad is removed and opens onto the table. Tilton scans each drawing, clearly impressed with every flip of the page. Remarkable. Richard is clearly a genius. Someone is coming. Tilton grabs the keys and rushes out.

THE VERRAZANO BRIDGE

The Verrazano-Narrows Bridge is a soaring expanse that links Brooklyn with Staten Island. At the foot of the bridge, on the Staten Island side, is the FDR Boardwalk, a quaint park alongside New York Harbor that's a haven to runners and cyclists. Elderly couples sit on benches staring at the sea and kids play on the swings as the gigantic Verrazano looms high above them.

Lying on the grass beside her parked Prius is Fiona Fitzgerald, 28, slender, pale, without make up or pretense, a tight pony tail accents the roundness of her face. She looks up to the cloudless blue sky, breathing slowly, trying to calm herself. Inhale. Exhale. Just be. Fiona thinks any of life's problems could easily be fixed through yoga, an avocado smoothie, or incense. This particular problem required yoga. She opens her eyes to see her brother Richard's face.

"How you doin' down there, Fiona?"

"I tried, Richie. I really did."

His sisters call him Richie. To the rest of the world he's known as Richard. Richard Fitzgerald. He turns his head toward the Verrazano.

"That is a big fuckin' bridge."

"Looks like a God damn dinosaur from down here," says Fiona, trying to calm herself.

Richard lies down beside her, first making sure the ground is clean enough for his tailored suit. They both stare up.

"You're right. It does look like a dinosaur from down here," he says.

She clasps her brother's hand and holds it to her chest.

"I didn't even know she was sick."

"Mom? You really think she would tell anyone? You know us Fitzgeralds. Gotta keep up appearances."

They both smile. Richard stares at the sky, reminiscing.

"She'd have me put on Izod shirts and crease my chinos just to go to Pathmark. Wouldn't want the cashier to think we couldn't afford the groceries, right?"

"And look at you now," says Fiona. "New York's top fashion designer."

"I used to be," he mutters softly.

Fiona turns to her brother with a concerned, sisterly look. He brushes it off, and yells to the sky with an Irish brogue.

"Tanks, Ma. I couldn't have done it without ye."

"Oh my God, you sounded just like Dad."

Richard gives a wink and a smile, just like his old man. "Come on. You're supposed to be my date."

"Of course. Appearances." Fiona sits up and brushes the grass off Richard's thousand-dollar suit jacket. "Can you imagine if Mom knew I was dating a black guy."

"That's probably what killed her," says Richard.

She playfully punches his arm. "You're awful. Wait, aren't you dating a black guy?"

"Puerto Rican. It's a US territory, so I'm thinking maybe mom would be OK with that."

They both laugh. She wouldn't be.

"Let's go before Theresa kills Dad and we're officially orphans."

Richard pulls his sister up and they walk to the car. He avoids stepping in the mud with his expensive shoes, she plods right through in her sandals.

****

Theresa sits behind the wheel of her aging Chevy Malibu. Beside her in the passenger seat is Gerry

Mahoney, her boyfriend of twelve years. Yep, twelve years. Gerry is a local cop with a heart as big as his frame, a six-foot-four two hundred fifty-pound Teddy bear. It's impossible not to love this simple guy. They both stare up at the red light, Theresa well on her way to being pissed off - again.

"Why did you have me take Colonial? This light takes forever."

Gerry is used to her moods and continues to stare dreamily at the lights.

"You know I've never been in a limousine?"

"We're gonna be late," she snaps.

"Kinda funny though, isn't it?" he asks to no one in particular.

"Funny? What's so funny, Gerry? Funny that I'm gonna miss my mother's service? Oh, she'd love that, wouldn't she?" Theresa imitates her mother's biting brogue. *"late again, are ye, Theresa? I knew it. Just like always."*

Gerry is silent, still contemplating, as Theresa continues her rant.

"Or, or is it funny that my brother and sister will be standing in the receiving line without me, the oldest. God, what's with these lights!"

"It's just funny how we'll get to run this," Gerry says calmly as if just realizing a fact.

"What the hell are you talking about?"

"Funeral processions get to drive through red lights. Which is kinda funny when you think about it. I mean, what's the rush, you know? It's...it's ironic."

Theresa is at a point in their relationship where she's used to his simple observations, but this is ridiculous.

Gerry continues, "I mean, you really only get to go in a limo for funerals...." He knows he's stepping onto thin ice. "...or bachelor parties..." The ice begins to crack around him. Careful, Gerry. Careful. "...or weddings." Theresa's eyes shoot daggers.

"Really? You're gonna do this now? Today?"

"Right. Sorry." They both wait in silence before he speaks up. "I'm just sayin'."

"Jesus, Gerry. My mother just died."

"Yes. Right. Sorry."

She's really not that sad - it's more of a deflection. She looks to the right at the opposing traffic light. Still green. No cars.

"Come on. Come on."

Tired of waiting, she hits the gas and runs the light. Again. A horn BLASTS and she SLAMS on the brakes, narrowly missing a passing car. It's a hearse. Their bodies rock back and they sit stunned for a beat.

Theresa finally speaks. "Now that's ironic."

STANTON FUNERAL HOME

The room is filled with somber people and an overpowering mixture of stale flowers and aftershave. Theresa rushes in, taking her place in the receiving line beside her brother and sister. Fiona gives her a warm embrace.

"Didn't think you'd show up," Richard says through the side of his mouth.

"Got caught at the lights."

"Seriously? That's your excuse?"

"Stop it, you two," snaps Fiona, always the peacemaker.

Gerry greets Richard with an overly dramatic, consoling bear hug, practically lifting him off his feet.

"Fitzy. I'm so sorry."

"It's Richard," he squeaks, wincing from Gerry's tight grasp. "It's OK, Gerry. Really. You can let go."

Richard always hated the name Fitzy. His family and a few old friends (only a few) call him Richie. His mother never did though. It was always Richard. As in, *What is wrong with you, Richard? Why can't you act like the other boys, Richard?* The nickname Fitzy makes his skin curl. Fitzy is a freckled kid who leans against a wall and spits through a gap in his teeth. Fitzy skates left wing on the Mite A hockey team. Fitzy drinks

Bud Lite (in cans) and smokes Marlboro Reds. Richard Fitzgerald has worked too hard to create an image and a name for himself. Michael Kors. Tommy Hilfiger. Ralph Lauren. 'Designs by Fitzy' just wouldn't seem to fit among the runways of Paris and Milan.

"How you holdin' up, Fitz? I mean, Richard. You good?" asks Gerry, really meaning it.

Richard answers with a canned, almost dismissive response. "Our Spring collection is running into shipment problems. The price of suede has tripled. We're behind in our new release. So, no Gerry, I'm not doing too 'good'."
His eyes scan Gerry's cheap, ill-fitting suit.

"You should really just use one button, Gerry. It slims the silo…Never mind."

Gerry proudly slides his fingers along his suit lapels.
"Pretty sweet, huh? Men's Wearhouse. Buy One, Get One."

"Good God. There are two of these?" Richard is appalled. Theresa, stepping in to deflect the sarcasm as Richard feigns innocence, looks at her brother and snaps,

"Stop being an asshole, Richie." She turns to Gerry, "Can you go find my father? Just like him to go missing."

Gerry gladly takes the search assignment. He's at his best when he's assigned chores. Packy run? Gerry's in the car. Start the grill? Gerry's on it. Light a fire? Gerry knows the best way to stack logs. Go get your father from the Pub so he can attend his wife's wake? Roger that. He takes off with purpose.

"OK. I'll see you guys in the limousine."

Richard leans to Theresa, "He knows there's no limo, right?"

"I haven't got the heart to tell him," Theresa says as they both watch him leave.

Shelagh Murphy approaches, 43, like her cousin Theresa only thicker and tougher but with fiery red hair. Shelagh isn't married and really could not give two shits about having a husband. She's perfectly happy in her pink, freckled Celtic skin. She approaches the Fitzgerald family and lovingly takes Theresa's hand with perfect gentleness and sympathy, as if she's about to give some mournful, impassioned words of support.

The two cousins stand face to face, looking deeply into each other's eyes.

"You've put on a tremendous amount of weight," says Shelagh.

"Tough time for that acne to flare up," replies Theresa.

"I slept with Gerry."

"I know. He said you really sucked in bed."

They give each other a sarcastic smile, then a loving hug - one that only tight cousins share.

"Sorry cuz," says Shelagh. "Everyone at work sends their condolences."

"Thanks, Murph."

Fiona watches the exchange with disgust, she's seen this before. Theresa turns to her sister.

"What? You want all the crying and shit? You know our family - we don't do sad."

Fiona begins to twist at a rubber band on her wrist – it's her nervous fidget.

"Yeah," she mutters under her breath. "I know."

KELLY'S TAVERN

As much as Michaleen loved his life in America, he hated the explosion and exploitation of the traditional Irish Pub. Kelly's is different. This is a local haunt, for the local gents from the neighborhood to sit and drink and shoot the bull. Serious men who do serious drinking. They don't serve beer in 'flights' or Cosmopolitans, and they're not in the mood for your fuckin' politics. Two men with fiddles and another with a small accordion sit beside a fake fireplace, reminding everyone that they're not in Ireland - they're in Brooklyn. Although, the walls are adorned with real Irish memorabilia, not ticky tacky 'Kiss Me I'm Irish' bullshit. Men sit on barstools nursing Guinness like it's their job.

The bartender, James "Biffo" Shaughnessy, 62, is a stout man with a strong chin, thick hair and a nose that draws a second look; the north of it goes left, the south bends to the right, clearly the work of pugilistic nights throwing men out of the place. Biffo tosses a bar rag over his shoulder and pulls at the tap.

"If it isn't Michaleen Christopher O'Connor Fitzgerald, himself. Game slayer. Ladies' man. Outlaw."

"'Tis indeed, Biffo. 'Tis indeed."

Michaleen has filled a lot into his 67 calendar years. Biffo was correct with the monikers of Game Slayer, Ladies man and Outlaw, along with philosophizer, fisherman, sometimes handyman, and stranger to his kids - all of which Michaleen has stubbornly confused with a sort of care free independence. He grabs a stool as Biffo pulls the bar towel from his shoulder, wipes the counter in front of him and plops down a foamy Guinness.

"I thought you was in Florida, Mick. Or maybe went back to Ireland."

"Ireland's cold and wet, Biff. A miserable place to quit drinking."

"You quit drinking?" asks Biffo as he pulls the glass away. Michaleen tries to repress a shudder but fails, quickly reaching for the lager and restoring world order.

"Don't be a feckin' eejit. The very thought of it. Did, ah, did anyone come 'round looking for me?" asks Michaleen with a hint of trepidation.

"No. Why? Someone's husband after you again?"

"Adultery is a young man's game. I'll be looking for a rich old woman with a cough, this time 'round."

"I was sorry to hear about Bridget, Mick," Biffo says with sincerity. Michaleen receives it as such, and they raise a glass. "To Bridget Murphy Fitzgerald."

The men at the bar join in. "Bridget."

Michaleen stares at his drink.

"I'll miss arguing with her. She gave it good, that one did," he says with almost a hint of sadness to his voice. "I may deny that tomorrow though. Well gents, guess I'm officially divorced."

The door opens, letting the light of day stream in as they all squint.

"Michaleen? Is Michaleen Fitzgerald in here?" Michaleen instinctively pushes his Go bag under his stool. Biffo responds to the dark silhouette.

"Who's asking?"

"Officer Gerald Mahoney. NYPD."

Gerry never misses an opportunity to introduce himself as a member of the New York Police Department. He loves Theresa, impatience and all, but he loves being a police officer more.

The patrons instinctively dummy up in silence. Whenever a stranger walked into Kelly's and called out a name, it could be one of three situations. One - a bookie looking for the person who owed money. Two - a husband looking for the guy that slept with his wife. Three - Immigration looking for illegal Irish. Michaleen usually hits two out of three - but in this particular instance, he was in the clear.

"Gerry, my good man," says a relieved Michaleen. "Come. Sit."

"I knew you'd be in here," Gerry says proudly, "I'm a cop, you know. NYPD."

"Are ye, now? And what, eh, what type of police work are ye on?" asks Mick.

"Just traffic stuff. For now. But I'm working my way towards detective. Maybe narcotics. I don't really know yet." Michaleen seems almost relieved.

"I was waitin' on a business associate. Thought you might be him."

Biffo interjects, "What kind of business you into these days, Mick?"

"Birth control device tester," he snaps back. "Some notable failures in the past. Theresa. Richard. Fiona. But, with the right amount of practice I'm getting better."

The men at the bar laugh. Gerry's face is full of confusion. He's always on the fringes of any conversation or joke.

"Speaking of Theresa," Gerry says, "she told me to come get you."

"Ah just one drink."

"I think she'll be mad if we don't come back soon, Mick."

"She's always mad, that one," says Michaleen.

"Actually, they all seemed kinda mad when I left," replies Gerry.

Michaleen rubs at the back of his neck and scrunches his face, genuinely troubled by Gerry's statement.

"Arguing again, those three. Fine. Fine. We best get back then before they kill each other."

In an effort to help, Gerry reaches for the Go bag below the barstool, but Michaleen jumps.

"No, no I got this."

Gerry stops. It's all a bit suspicious.

Michaleen begins to pat himself down. Keys. Teeth. No wallet. He leans in close to Gerry and whispers, "Be a good lad and pay the man, will ye Gerry? I'm still in mourning."

Another chore for Gerry. He's happy to do it.

****

The family gathers in the side office of the Stanton Funeral Home, a dingy room, full of heavy, dark, ornate furniture. Richard constantly checks his watch, one leg squeezed firmly over the other, his arms snapped tight across his chest, appalled by the decor. Fiona, always the sensitive one, the baby of the family, dabs at a tear. Theresa scans the room for her father and Gerry, her mood swinging from impatience to anger.

Funeral director Henry Stanton is ensconced in a leather chair behind an enormous oak desk, his perfectly coifed white hair slicked straight back from his forehead. Mr. Stanton is probably one of the last remaining men to have an Ajax plastic comb always in his pocket and a tube of Brill cream at the ready. He clears his throat, gives a solemn look to the family seated in the room, and begins the presentation he's done thousands of times.

"I am very sorry for your loss."

A murmur of polite thank you's.

"At Stanton we pride ourselves with giving the utmost care and services for your loved ones in this time of need."

Fiona interrupts. "Wait. I'm sorry. Shouldn't we wait for Dad?"

Richard looks at his watch, "I need to get to the city."

"You're not coming back to the house?" Fiona pleads. He can see she needs him to be there.

"Yes. Of course."

"Go on," says Theresa. "We don't need to wait."

Stanton tries to regain control of the room. "Very well. Now. Who will be responsible for the ashes?"

There is noted silence. All eyes turn to Theresa.

"Don't look at me."

Richie shoots back, "I just had the whole apartment redone. It's a Jeffrey Bilhuber design."

"Like we know who that is - or give a shit," Theresa volleys. They both look at Fiona sitting nervously, twisting at the rubber band on her wrist. She's a no.

The door swings open and Michaleen hurries into the room with Gerry in tow. Mick instructs Gerry to sit down in the back, so as not to intrude, in one of the creaky, nimble chairs, causing Mr. Stanton to wince.

"Whad'I miss?" asks Michaleen.

The tension in the room is thick. "Thanks for showing up, Dad," Theresa snipes.

Stanton speaks up. "We were just discussing the transfer of ashes."

"Well I'm not takin' the jar," says Michaleen, "I had her with me the whole ride from Florida."

Stanton produces a colored brochure from inside his desk.

"Technically, it's...it's not a jar. It's an urn. Handcrafted classic with a brushed gold finish. A fine vessel, really. If it's the style you object to, we offer a wide selection of..."

Theresa doesn't wait for the full sales pitch, and interrupts. "It's not the vessel that's the problem. It's where we're gonna dock it." Her biting tone giving them all pause.

Richie breaks the frosty silence. "I think it would look great on the mantle in the living room."

"Are you fucking serious? I'm not putting it on the mantle."

"Theresa, watch yer language," commands Michaleen.

"Really?" she glares back. "You're gonna step up and parent now?"

That shuts him up. Richie tries again. "She should be in her house."

"It's my house now," volleys Theresa.

"You wanted to live there."

"And you didn't!"

She's right. Richie couldn't wait to get out of that tiny neighborhood, and all of Brooklyn. Fiona, the peacemaker again, breaks her silence. "Stop you two. Just stop!"

Michaleen shakes his head, deeply troubled by his kids fighting and the effortless way they all slip back into family routines and bitterness. Something has to be done.

Stanton raises a hand to catch the attention of one of his employees just outside the doorway. A large man in a dark suit, black rain coat and enormous shoes exits to retrieve something.

The room is eerily quiet as the family sits brooding in silence, until the sound of rattling china can be heard from beyond the door. The employee returns, anxious, walking gingerly, hands shaking as he carries the urn bearing their mother's ashes. They're all terrified he's going to drop it.

He just about trips as he enters but catches himself. Holy shit that was close! Gerry, of course, leaps from the nimble chair and tries to catch the poor soul. Good old Gerry. Part hero. Part Cop. All heart.

The employee regains his composure and continues the shaky journey. There's a collective sigh of relief when the urn is finally placed on Stanton's desk, and the employee walks off.

"Sorry about that," Stanton says reassuringly. "He's pretty shaken up. Someone ran a red light this morning and almost hit him."

All eyes land in Theresa. She grabs the urn.

"Fine. I'll take it," she snaps, and turns to Richard, "but you're paying for the service."

"What? I'm…" He stops. He knows he can't win this battle.

"Fine."

As they all stand to leave, Michaleen begins to go through his ritual. Back pocket. Front pocket. Lips. Thinking it's some sort of Irish prayer, Mr. Stanton awkwardly attempts to bless himself.

Theresa looks at her puzzled siblings.

"Don't ask."

BAY RIDGE, NEW YORK

The house is dark and quiet, a nice respite from a day of family bickering and an evening of entertaining people in the living room. Theresa sits alone in the kitchen staring at the urn that sits atop a worn Formica table. The surrounding countertops are jam packed with foil-covered casserole dishes, cake tins and bakery boxes. It's an interesting thing about funerals - people bake and cook and bring food as if it somehow relieves all the grief. Bridget used to say, *all the Irish think they're Italian and bring baked ziti, and all the Italians eat the chicken salad sandwiches.*

Richard quietly enters, still looking sharp in his tailored suit, and leans against the sink.

"You two want to be alone?"

"Very funny," Theresa replies. "Couldn't sleep. I'm usually doing rounds at this hour."

"I'm usually buying rounds at this hour."

He smirks and joins his sister at the table.

"Where's Dad?"

"The porch."

"Let me guess. He likes the view."

They both give a knowing smile.

"How long's he staying?" asks Richard.

"Your guess is as good as mine. No luggage. Just a backpack he calls his 'Go bag'"

Richard picks up and inspects the urn closely, almost admiring its craftsmanship.

"Honestly?" he deadpans. "I think it looks really great here. Kind of goes with the whole 'Shabby Irish chic' decor."

They finally crack smiles.

"That was quite a scene today."

She nods. "It sure was."

She stands and reaches for a bottle of cheap whiskey she keeps hidden above the fridge. It's mostly there for tougher than usual shifts at the hospital.

"You, ah, you don't happen to have any single malt around?" asks Richard.

Theresa shoots him a look. That's a no. She pours her cheap brown whiskey into two coffee mugs.

"Your life is just one boulevard of green lights, isn't it" she says with biting sarcasm. He gets it. He can be a real pretentious prick sometimes.

"So...how's the world of high fashion?"

Richard stares into his mug. "You're only as good as your last design. And, sister dear, it's been a while since I've had a hit. Seems every time I come up with a new idea, someone already has it."

Theresa has a genuine look of concern on her face. He gives her a reassuring look back.

"Stop. I'm fine."

"Really?" She means it.

"Yes. I'm sure."

Theresa isn't convinced. Even though they have their fights and differences, she's still the big sister. And now with Bridget gone, she's realizing she has to be the mother too.

"How's Fiona doing?"

"The same," he replies.

They both look concerned, and drink in silence.

"You know her," says Theresa trying to minimize everything. "All life's problems can be fixed through yoga and some John Tesh music."

Richie swirls the whiskey in his coffee mug. "Yeah, well, maybe she knows something we don't." They both think on that. Maybe she does. Richard takes a sip from his mug, and is immediately disgusted.

****

Fiona unpacks her overnight bag in the tiny bedroom that was once hers. Not much has changed in the years since she grew up there. The patterned wallpaper is curling up in corners. A folded afghan blanket lays across the foot of the single bed. Fiona was the baby of the family, and always sort of lived in the background, listening, taking everything in.

As a girl she was quiet, not shy, she just chose not to say much, observing her surroundings. Now in her twenties, she's grown to be more confident. But, standing in that room she's the frightened quiet little girl who used to sit on the edge of her bed and listen to her family quarrel and bicker downstairs. Through the holes in the floor by the old cast iron radiator she could hear everything that was said in the kitchen. It's where she learned that they weren't getting a dog, even though Michaleen had promised they could get one. *And who do you think will be taking care of it?* It's where she learned that Richie didn't want to play hockey anymore. Or any sports, for that matter. *There's got to be something wrong with a boy your age not playing sport. What will everyone think of that?* It's where she would listen to Theresa and her mother argue. Their fights were epic, hitting every note and tempo.

Nagging. Screaming. Passive-aggressing sniping. Door slamming. Every situation was a pretext for confrontation. The wrong clothes. Not enough clothes. Hair too long. Too much make-up. Not enough make up. Music too loud. *Get out of the kitchen...again, Theresa.* Bridget would snarl, mocking the angry teenager's struggle with weight. It's how she learned about her father's indiscretions. And her mother's hurt. And it's where she could hear her brother and sister downstairs talking about her, *"Maybe she knows something we don't."* Asking each other, *"How's Fiona doing?"* Words that would always waft through the house. *"How's Fiona doing?"* *"She seems better, doesn't she?"* Out there in the world, away from Bay Ridge, Fiona is a well-respected Art Teacher at a school for children on the autism spectrum. It's a job that requires kindness, creativity, listening skills, and most of all patience. Everything not found in her youth and in that house. But now there, in that room, she's thirteen-year-old scared, anxious, overly sensitive Fiona. Nothing here felt right.

On a dark oak dresser in an imitation silver frame is a photo of three teenagers: Richie looking dapper in an Izod shirt and creased chinos. Plump Theresa squeezed into an outfit she obviously didn't choose for herself. Gangly, pale Fiona, with long, straight, greasy hair giving a forced smile. Standing sentry over this trio in the picture is middle-aged Bridget Murphy Fitzgerald. Plain. No makeup. No smile.

Just an impatient look that seems to say, "take the picture already, Michaleen." Her hands are firmly clenched on the kids shoulders in an effort to control and corral. Fiona solemnly rubs a thumb over the photo, thinking about their family dynamic and how such different people could possibly be related by blood.

Fiona begins to rub and fidget with the rubber band on her wrist. Her heartbeat begins to throb in her ears. She tells herself, breathe Fiona, find your Zen. But she is turning pale. The confident creative Art Teacher is the quiet, gangly teenager again. She closes her eyes and sees police lights flash. A stretcher is wheeled out a front door towards an ambulance waiting in the street. Neighbors look on with concern and judgement.

She shakes off the memory, regains composure, then spills the remaining contents of her overnight bag onto the bed; Meditation books. Himalayan oils. Pill bottles of Adderall, Lexapro, Valium. She pops a few, gulps water, and turns off the light.

****

Theresa shuffles into the kitchen slowly, nursing her head from the cheap whiskey she shared with Richie last night, and waits on the coffee maker. Fiona bounces in, a rolled yoga mat under her arm and healthy green smoothie in hand.

"Good morning," she chirps.

"You sleep on that thing?" growls Theresa.

"Meditation. You should try it."

Fiona takes a seat across from her at the table, her energy so annoying Theresa just wants to punch her in the face. Fiona can feel it.

"You know, Theresa, happiness comes from within. It's not what's around you. It's what's inside you."

"I need coffee inside me."

"You know what you need?" asks Fiona.

"I can't wait to hear."

"The cow in the parking lot."

Theresa looks at her sister. "What the fuck?"

"It's a Zen approach to overcoming anger."

"You know what makes me angry? Talking before coffee." Theresa raps at the side of the coffee maker. That's it. No more percolator. She's getting a Keurig.

"It's a parable." Says Fiona. "Buddhism and meditation are all about transformation. Close your eyes."

Theresa hesitates.

"Come on."

"Will it make you shut up?" asks Theresa.

"Close your eyes. Go on."

Fiona waits, insisting. Theresa shuts her eyes, reluctantly.

"The goal is to not move or think or feel. Just be. Get out of your head. Now, imagine you're driving in a crowded parking lot, circling, when, just as you spot a space, another driver races ahead and takes it."

"This isn't helping Fiona," deadpans Theresa, eyes shut tight.

"It's easy to imagine the rage, right?" asks Fiona. "But now imagine that instead of another driver, a cow has lumbered into that parking space and settled down. The anger dissolves into bemusement. What really changed? You? Or your perspective. See?"

"All I see is a dead cow and a dented front bumper. Gonna cost me two hundred bucks, plus insurance points. Nice job, Fi."

Fiona gives up. Theresa opens her eyes to see Michaleen enter from the porch, carrying the urn.

"Now I really have rage. Will you sleep inside, for Chrissake Dad? It's embarassing."

"To who?" asks Micheleen. "That little shit machine Flanagan dog? Besides, I can see the stars from out there."

Fiona gives her father a morning kiss. She was always Daddy's little girl.

"A better view, right Dad?"

"That's right, baby girl. Glad one of yiz was listening. I already started breakfast, so go on and sit. All of yiz."

Fiona peers over his shoulder as he stirs the frying pan on the aging, yellowing stove. "Is...is that sausage?"

"Black pudding," says Mick.

"I don't eat meat, Dad."

"It's not meat. It's blood." He looks her frail figure up and down. "You could use the color."

She turns even more pale. "I'll just make tea."

Theresa, finally with coffee in hand, says, "I know a parking lot where we could get some steaks."

The door swings and in comes Richard, looking like he just walked out of a magazine - a tailored jacket, white shirt, high collar, expensive slacks and suede shoes. And checking his watch, like always.

"Where ye off to, then?" asks Michaleen.

"Back to the city."

"Not so fast. Got some business to discuss with all of yiz."

"I'm not sitting in traffic back to Manha.."

Michaleen shoots him a look. It's "the look" - the one every kid knows. The one that comes right before a SMACK to the head. Richie and Theresa knew it. They were always on the receiving end. Mostly Theresa, though. She could never hold her tongue, always with the quick word or snide remark from the back of the car, and before she knew it, a hand would fly from the front seat. *You watch how you speak to your father.*

Richard slowly sits down, joining his sisters at the table, as Michaleen dishes the food onto plates and breakfast is placed in front of them. Fiona gags a bit at the sight of the burnt blood sausage.

"There now. Isn't this nice?" says a smiling Michaleen.

They sit crammed at the small table. When they were kids everything was a recipe to start a fight here. Encroachment. An elbow bump. A foot kick. A comment about one's attire. Everything was fair game until "the look" quieted them all down.

"Now, this business about yer mother's ashes."

All three protest.

"I'm not gonna…"

"No way am taking that…"

"Daddy, I can't…"

"Enough!" says Michaleen with 'the look' again. He takes the urn from the table and begins to pry off the top.

"Jesus Christ!"

"Are you insane?"

"Daddy, no!"

A glare. Silence. Dad's in charge.

"Your mother left instructions."

"There's more?" asks Theresa sarcastically.

"Yes, there's more. And these are important."

Michaleen reaches into the urn. Fiona looks as if she'll faint. Theresa and Richard give each other a "What the hell is he doing?" look as Michaleen pulls out three colored plastic baggies. Each one is placed on the table in order; RED for Theresa. GREEN for Richard. YELLOW for Fiona.

"Subtle," scoffs Theresa. The symbolism is not lost on her.

"What the hell are we supposed to do with these?" asks Richard.

Michaleen dons his glasses and begins to read from the note, the same note he read to Theresa earlier but didn't finish.

"And these are my final wishes. Each child is to dispose of my ashes at a specific location."

He hands each a sealed envelope. Theresa is growing suspicious.

"Let me see that note."

Michaleen quickly pulls it away.

"Ah, ah. Back off, Missy. You all know how your mother demanded order. Appearances, and the like. She was…"

"Controlling?" says Theresa.

"Manipulative?" says Richard.

"Stop it," says Fiona the peacemaker. "Go on Daddy." Michaleen regains control.

"I was going to say, organized. Now, these were her wishes - a mother's final wishes - and there is nothing more sacred. Or binding."

He removes his glasses and addresses them, looking each child in the eye because he means business. "You're each going to take the bags, and you're going to follow the instructions in that envelope - or God help us she'll curse us all."

Silence fills the room. Bridget Fitzgerald was all those things. Manipulative. Judgmental. Organized. It was just like her to plan out these directives, exacting a toll on the children to fill out her orders just so she could maintain control even after she was gone. Besides, she always did have a flair for exits. It all makes sense, in a morbid, angry kind of way. Reluctantly, but dutifully, they all know they must do this.

A knock at the door breaks the silence. It's Gerry, a case of beer on his shoulder.

"Morning, all. I mean, good morning, not good 'mourning'. You guys know that, right?" Big lug, he always struggles to get words right.

"I thought I'd fill the coolers in case more people showed up today."

"Brilliant," says Michaleen. "Theresa, you've my permission to marry this man."

Gerry spies the sausages on the table. "Anybody gonna eat this? No?" He happily shovels them in, oblivious to the mood of the room. He could eat anything, at any time.

Theresa rolls her eyes, not ready to respond. Not ready to embrace any of this just yet. Her hangover is still kicking in, she's slowing coming to the realization that she has to dump a third of her mother's ashes somewhere, and now her fucking coffee is cold.

The Fitzgerald children sit in silence and stare at the three colored baggies on the table in front of them. A good mourning indeed.

BRIDGET AND MICHALEEN

Bridget Murphy and Michaleen Fitzgerald met in the summer of 1972, both in their twenties, both new to America and both finding their footing in New York. Michaleen was as gregarious as Bridget was shy; as boastful as she was drilled in modesty. Her strict Irish Catholic upbringing would never allow for bragging or, God forbid, any sign of showy happiness. Michaleen was everything she wasn't and in many ways that's what probably drew her to him. Their marriage ran the typical course from curiosity and polite pleasantries to long stretches of impatience and argument. They seemed stuck together out of habit or boredom, and over time any semblance of love just simply disappeared altogether. Bridget was too busy raising the children (controlling them) to ever imagine any other alternative. There may have been a laundry list of reasons why she married Michaleen in the first place, but not one of them had anything to do with love. Their meeting, a haphazard courtship, their years raising Theresa, Richard and

Fiona, all of it was done to keep up the appearance of a happy family. Her rigid stubbornness and his wandering eye were the only constants, and in the end, they just succeeded in making each other miserable. Bridget was far too proud and far too Catholic to ever grant Michaleen a divorce. While Michaleen had the capacity to make everyone around him feel better, Bridget was an orchestra of self-absorption. Starchy. Furious. Uncompromising. She wasn't happy unless she was trying to change people and trying to change Michaleen was at the top of her list.

In fairness, Michaleen hadn't fallen out of love with her so much as he'd become disillusioned with the strict rigidity of matrimony. Love. Honor. Obey. Mick wasn't much for rules. If he didn't follow the Ten Commandments, he sure as hell wasn't about to obey the hundred or more from his wife. The instructions, given to each of the children and written in her flowing cursive Catholic school penmanship, may be the only orders Bridget ever gave Michaleen that he would obey willingly and without argument.

★★★★

Michaleen spent close to thirty years climbing poles all over the five burroughs for New York Bell, first stringing phones lines, then cable, then computer coaxial wires. It was a job that paid the bills at home (sometimes) and at Kelly's

Tavern. But it was fishing that he loved. Three nights a week and on weekends he would somehow find the water. When he was offered early retirement, the first stop he made was to the boat yard. Well, maybe not the first stop…he had a few celebratory drinks at Kelly's first, then he went boat shopping. But he was of sound mind and faculty when he pulled the trigger and used his severance on a thirty-five-foot Chris-Craft. When he drove up with the boat in tow, right there in front of the house for all the neighbors to see, the look on Bridget's face made him wished he'd stayed at the bar.

Maybe moving to Florida might make her happy, or at least get them both out of the cold New York winters. "We are island people," Michaleen told her. "First the Emerald Island. Then Long Island. And now Marco Island. It'll be grand." With that brogue and those twinkling blue eyes, he could talk anyone into anything. Truth be told, Michaleen's philandering was legendary, and Bridget was more than happy to get a thousand miles away from all the gossip and petty innuendo. *Why the hell I ever let your father talk me into moving to this God forsaken state, I'll never know,* Bridget would complain to Theresa. (Among other things like all the foreigners, the heat, old people, the heat, slow drivers, the heat.) So, they bought a condo and moved. Six months later

and free from the neighborhood gossipers like Rose
Flanagan, Bridget finally had the confidence to kick him out.

She lived by herself, and she was fine with that. The
solitude gave her time to be alone with her thoughts and her
memories - and her silent regrets. She was alone when she
found the lump in her armpit. Alone when the doctor gave
her the short, rapid timeline. But she was with Michaleen
when she sat at the table and wrote the notes to her three
children in flowing cursive penmanship. She was far too
proud to let anyone know of her demise. She didn't want pity
or lengthy sob stories, and she certainly wasn't going back to
New York looking frail and ill - her vanity would never allow
that. Fitzgeralds don't do sad. Fitzgeralds keep up
appearances. In the end, it made sense that the only way she
would ever return to Brooklyn was in a jar a box or colored
plastic baggies.

RICHARD FITZGERALD

Richard's gorgeous contemporary apartment over looks Manhattan's Upper West Side. The rooms are filled with high end art and expensive furniture with meticulous attention to detail. Richard sits on a white leather couch with a tumbler of scotch. Macallan 25. Retail price $1,980 - something Richard is sure to let everyone know whenever he pours them a glass.

He scans the latest fashion magazines, looking troubled by the images and the headline that reads: **MARCO PACELLI A SMASH HIT IN MILAN.** A key opens the front door and in walks Eduardo Perez, Richard's handsome Puerto Rican boyfriend. His heavy accent is overshadowed only by his heavy attitude.

"Why do you not take my calls?"

"Tilton was screening them."

"And he screens me out? I don't like this Tilton," only with his heavy accent it comes out Teel-ton.

"He's a good kid," says Richard.

"He's leetle chit."

He stops, looks at Richard and gives a caring smile. "I was concerned. And your sister? She is doing better?"

"She seems OK."

"And you?" asks Eduardo concerned.

"I'm fine."

Eduardo gives him a look. He waits.

"I'm fine, Eduardo. Really."

"You Americans, you're so bottled up. Puerto Ricans. We are emotional. Compassionate. Expressive. Loud."

Richard pours himself another glass of Macallan.

"Yeah, well, my family is none of those things. Except loud."

He holds up the magazine he'd been reading. Eduardo sees his face, defeated.

"I was hoping you didn't see that."

"I've been working on this concept for months!" Richard says with a slam of the magazine onto the couch. "Pony tailed little freak. The man hasn't had a decent collection since the 90's."

Eduardo sits beside him, trying to calm his mood, when he spots the green bag of ashes on the coffee table. He grabs it in disbelief.

"And so you are turning to drugs to deal with this?"

Richard replies nonchalantly. "It's my mother."

"Again with your mother. My mother didn't love me. She was cold. She was judgmental. She didn't pick me up after baseball practice. You need to let it go, Richard. All this anger is going to..."

"I'm talking about the bag. Those are my mother's ashes."

Eduardo drops the baggie as if he were electrocuted, then blesses himself. "Dios mío! And...and why is she here? She should be in an urn on our mantle."

"Seriously?" quips Richard as he scans the newly refurbished apartment. No way a tacky brass urn is going to fit into this decor. Eduardo agrees, and deadpans. "Maybe you are right."

Richard goes back to his scotch. "We're supposed to scatter them."

"Scatter. What is this word, 'scatter'?

"We each have instructions."

He removes the envelope from his jacket pocket. Even in the comfort of his home, sipping Macallan 25 on his own leather couch, Richard is still dressed sharp in a blazer. One button. Always one button.

Eduardo opens the envelope and reads the notecard:
Richard 40.655509 -73.604247

"This is a phone number? A church maybe?"

"I have no idea. Honestly, I can't be bothered with cryptic instructions from my dead mother."

The clothes. The apartment. Richard has built a world of absurd wealth, surrounding him like a suit of armor. He had always been tortured by self- doubt, allowing other people's opinions about him to trump his own, that's how he learned to create such popular, trendsetting stylish designs. And now he sits in constant fear of losing it all, losing his edge. To Marco Pacelli of all people.

"Why do you care so much what people think?" asks Eduardo.

"Those 'people' are the ones that follow my designs. They pay for this apartment. They buy me this one thousand nine hundred eighty-five-dollar scotch."

"Yes, I know," snaps Eduardo. "And your expensive clothes, and your custom shoes, and your fine watch."

Richard fiddles with the knobs. "It's not a watch. It's a Patek Philippe."

Eduardo tenderly puts a hand over Richard's wrist. "Stop. Stop checking your watch and look at me."

After a moment, Richard finally looks up. Eduardo always knows how to melt his sharp exterior.

"You must do this, Richard. You must, what is the word? Scatter them. Esta es el deseo de una madre. It is a mother's wish."

"I know. Or else she'll put a curse on us," Richard says in an Irish brogue.

"Si. *La maldición,*" says Eduardo blessing himself.

This is why Richard fell in love with him. His passion. His emotion. His caring - feelings Richard never experienced growing up. He softens and interlocks his fingers with Eduardo.

"She'd like you. Your skin isn't as pale and freckled as she would have liked…but at least you're Catholic."

They both smile. Eduardo buries his head into Richard's shoulder.

"You must do this, Richard. All of you. Together."

Richard contemplates the idea.

"All of us together, huh? Now that would be a curse."

FIONA FITZGERALD

Fiona walks up the stairs to her Staten Island apartment, the tension of her family visit falling off with each step. The disheveled one-bedroom loft is a stark contrast to her brother's magnificent West Side living quarters. She's home, and so much more relaxed amid the clutter and chaos of her many unfinished paintings laying against the brick walls. Bridget Fitzgerald never fully appreciated Fiona's creative side. She had no patience for poetry, or flowery art, or the cacophony of today's music. *Turn that foolishness off.* And God help you if you ever used the term "starving artist" around a woman of Irish descent. *Those people have a choice. Your great-grandparents didn't.* Saying this as if Theresa, Richard and Fiona were singularly responsible for the great Irish famine.

Fiona kicks off her shoes, drops her overnight bag by the sink and checks the mail. She pours a glass of wine, and beams at the sight of her boyfriend Corey asleep on the couch. His sculpted muscular body a reflection of their organic vegan lifestyle. Fiona studies him lying there, a book dog eared across his chest, glasses on his forehead, noting how different he is from her in every way - and that's a good thing. He's calm, confident and smart.

She kneels quietly beside him and traces the outline of a Zen symbol tattooed on his arm. He told her it represented inner peace and tranquility. She saw that inner peace in his deep brown eyes and was jealous of his carefree attitude and devotions - and she fell hopelessly in love. She kisses him awake.

"Mmmm. Hey babe," says Corey blinking his eyes awake.

"Hey," she whispers back.

"Why didn't you tell me about the service? I would have gone with you."

"I have no intention of inflicting my family on you. Not yet, anyways. Besides, I had a date."

"Really? Should I be jealous?" he says with a slight hint of jealousy.

"It was my brother. You know he's gay, right?"

"Doesn't everyone?"

"Apparently, not my aunts."

Corey is confused. "My mother did her best not to let anyone know. She wasn't very, I'm searching for the right word...accepting. She had very strong opinions, and, well, I think she cared too much what the outside world thought."

Corey playfully pulls her on top of him. "She made you, so she must have been incredible. Tell me something about her."

Fiona kisses him. They fit together perfectly there on the couch.

"Like what?"

"I don't know. Like, what was her favorite time of day? Favorite candy? Did she let you open your presents on Christmas Eve, or did she make you wait until Christmas morning? Little things like that will help you keep her memory alive."

Fiona removes the rubber band from her wrist. She doesn't need it. She's home. It's her safe place.

"I'm not so sure I want to," she mutters, only half kidding.

"What?"

"Nothing. Can we talk about something else, like how I almost made it to the bridge? But, well then...Richie met me."

"Richie, huh? Not 'Richard Fitzgerald'?" mocks Corey "Well, that is a big fucking bridge."

"I know, right?" she exclaims. He pulls her close.

"I'm sorry about your mother. I love you."

"I love you, too."

It's comfortable, natural. He rolls off the couch and heads to the kitchen, which isn't really a kitchen as much as there's a sink and a fridge in this part of the apartment.

"You hungry? I can make us a smoothie."

"Starving. Hey, you ever eat blood sausage?

"No. But I ate monkey once when I was in Cameroon," he says as he opens the cabinets and pulls down an assortment of powders in plastic bags. Flax seed. Protein powder. Whey. He grabs a measuring cup and begins to place the powders into a blender.

"And I kissed you!?" mocks Fiona.

"I've brushed my teeth since then."

Thinking it's more healthy powder, Corey reaches for the plastic yellow baggie on the counter. Fiona yells from across the room.

"Oh my God. Stop!" She rushes over. "Sorry. That's…it's…it's ashes. From the funeral home."

"Really?" Corey looks closely at the bag, totally intrigued. "Cool. Although, technically it's not ash. It's broken down calcium phosphate. Maybe some other minerals like sodium, potassium. Basically, it's the same ingredient you'd find in table salt."

Fiona is a little embarrassed by it all.

"We're all supposed to scatter them at certain locations. Me, Richie and Theresa. My mother left instructions. These are mine."

She hands him the envelope with a note card:

FIONA 40.609445 -74.028543

"These look like coordinates," says Corey. "Latitude and longitude. Plug them into Google map."

Fiona begins to type the numbers into her phone. A puzzled look forms on her face. This can't be right.

Corey is busy with a smoothie creation, dumping the protein powders and flax seed into the blender.

"The funeral industry in the United States is one of the most expensive and bureaucratic in the world. Did you know, in the Philippines, for example, the Benguet tribe blindfold their dead and place them next to the main entrance of the house."

"Ew," Fiona grimaces.

"I know, right. The Tinguians dress the bodies in their best clothes, sit them on a chair and place a lit cigarette in their lips."

"Stop. The whole idea of this creeps me out."

"The world is running out of burial space. Cremation is a very popular alternative, and frankly, more civilized," Corey says preparing to mix the concoction. "If you think about it, your mother performed a very caring, unselfish act"

Fiona mutters to herself, "You obviously never met my mother."

He hits the blender - WHHHIIRRRR - and the powders and ice mix together.

THERESA FITZGERALD

Theresa and Gerry sit on the couch. Wine for her. Beer for him. Pizza for both. They didn't become boyfriend and girlfriend so much as they just fell into the habit of being together. Dinner at The Bridgeview Diner on Tuesdays. Bowling at Melody Lanes Thursdays. And rather than spend Saturday nights alone watching old John Wayne movies (the greatest American actor that ever lived. Nobody was cooler. Nobody. And they would both argue to the death to anyone who disagreed), they just started going over each other's house and nonchalantly called it Date Night. Tonight, they're at Gerry's, or rather, Gerry's mother's house. Like Theresa, he took over the mortgage since the real estate market in Brooklyn made everything way out of their price range.

Gerry always had a thing for Theresa, even when they were teenagers in the neighborhood. He was drawn to her toughness and smart as a whip sense of humor. Eventually, Theresa decided she liked him too. Like, *liked him,* liked him. And for twelve years they've had the same routine, comfortable like an old Lazy Boy recliner that just fits you perfectly. And it's so comfortable, why would you ever go look for another one? You'd have to spend all that time breaking it in.

She notices Gerry is a bit distant as they watch one of their all-time favorite John Wayne and Maureen O'Hara classics, THE QUIET MAN on television.

"What's wrong? This is your favorite movie."

He shrugs.

"Are you still upset I didn't tell you about the limo?"

"No. Well, yes." Gerry is hurt. This big lug of a guy can never hide his feelings.

He turns and looks at Theresa. "Can I ask you something? The other day at the service...I mean, you didn't even cry."

Theresa's taken aback. "What? I...I'm sad. I don't need to cry and shit."

"I know, but. I don't think I've ever seen you cry. Like, ever."

"Fitzgeralds don't do sad," she replies blankly, like it's a known fact and she's said it a hundred times before.

"But...you only have one mother." He waits. "Do you want to talk about it?"

"Talk about what?" she asks.

"The elephant in the room."

"Jesus. Not you too with the Zen bullshit. Have you been talking to Fiona?"

"Fiona? No. Why?"

Theresa is getting agitated. Gerry's confused. "You're mother's ashes are sitting in a plastic bag on your kitchen table. You think maybe that means something?"

Theresa continues to stare at the television. Gerry treads cautiously, knowing he's stepping out onto thin ice. "Maybe you haven't scattered the ashes because…because you need her in some way."

She turns to face him. "Need her? My mother? I didn't need her when she was alive, why would I need her now that she's dead?" She waits before she speaks, or in this case deflects. "Besides, I'm waiting on Richie and Fiona. We all agreed to do it together."

Gerry knows this is a stall tactic. So does Theresa. Suddenly, his cell phone rings.

"We're not done here," he says rearing back and pulling the phone from his pocket.

"Yeah. We are," she states firmly, and means it too. "Answer your phone, Dr. Phil."

Gerry puts the phone to his ear.

"Hi Ma. Yes, you know I'm with Theresa. My mother says, hello."

Theresa speaks with canned enthusiasm. "Hello Mrs. Mahoney."

Gerry's mother is calling from upstairs. She always calls. When she fell a few years ago and broke her hip, Gerry bought her a cell phone so she could always reach him – anytime, anywhere. He really beat himself up over her fall. *I should have put more salt down on the front steps.* No Emergency Lifeline button for her. She wants to speak to her son, her only son, Gerry and right now. In fact, he's numbers 1 through 4 on her speed dial list. #1 Gerry's cell. #2 Gerry's work. #3 Gerry's squad car. #4 Gerry's Captain - in case Gerry doesn't answer calls 1 through 3. The Captain just *loves* when Mrs. Mahoney calls and asks where Officer Mahoney is, and then spends fifteen minutes asking why her son hasn't been promoted yet.

Francine Mahoney always resented being left alone upstairs in her room during 'date night', and tonight was no exception. Gerry's trying too hard to make up the cheeriness.

"Of course she's happy you called, Mom. I know, I know. You'd make a great Grandmother, Mom. Someday. Just not right now."

Theresa rolls her eyes with undisguised irritation. Gerry is getting the 'I'm not going to live forever, you know' speech. Honestly, she may live forever just to torture Theresa.

Gerry continues to listen, trying to be patient.

"Do you need anything up there? Um, THE QUIET MAN. Yep, John Wayne was the best."

He laughs hard at something she says. Theresa is jealous. It's the kind of easy conversation she never had with her own mother.

"Yes. Ok. I love you too, Mom."

He hangs up, all aglow. Theresa waits before striking.

"What was all that about grandchildren?"

"She just wants me to be happy."

He waits. "Are you?"

"Am I what?"

"Happy."

"Can we just watch the movie please?" says an already annoyed Theresa.

"I'm serious. Are you happy?"

"Wine. Pizza. John Wayne and Maureen O'Hara." She looks back to the television, trying anything to avoid a deeper conversation. "What's not to be happy about?'

Gerry is still looking at her, wanting to go deeper.

"Am I doing it wrong? Am I supposed to get down on one knee? Bring flowers? Play music?'

"No. I..I don't know," she says, getting flustered. "Why can't we just do what we're doing? It works for Fiona and Corey."

"Yeah, so does sushi and powdered drinks," he says looking at his round belly. He flicks the television to mute. "Can we at least talk about it?"

Now Theresa is getting angry, but Gerry's just too sweet, too caring, to get her really pissed off. She grabs the remote from his hand, clicks the volume back on and tries to get them both back to watching the movie. "Come on. This is the best part."

Feeling guilty, she lays her head on his shoulder. Her eyes scan the room and stop at a wall of framed photos beyond the television; young Gerry in various stages stares back at her. Mrs. Mahoney has every school picture of her son from kindergarten through high school neatly arranged in succession. Gap-toothed, pre-braces Gerry. Full-braces Gerry. Awkward, pimply Gerry. Chubby pink-cheeked Gerry.

Too much hair gel Gerry. Crew cut Gerry. She nuzzles her head in closer to his chest, realizing how much history they've shared. She loves Gerry. All the Gerrys. Why can't she just tell him?

At the base of the wall is an end table with an assortment of Hummels alongside cheap knick knacks. In the middle is a strategically placed circle of ceramic animals. A kitten. A puppy. A seal with a ball on its nose. And there it is. Jesus Christ, she thinks to herself, there actually *is* an elephant in the room.

She should probably apologize, say something kind, romantic, loving - but she doesn't. She just stares at the television and tells him, "We'll see."

They continue to watch the movie in silence as John Wayne drags Maureen O'Hara across the rolling green Irish countryside.

MANHATTAN

Tilton sits at Richard's desk, hands behind his head and feet propped up. He's getting way too comfortable. He looks around the room and imagines his life as a famous fashion designer. He could do this. Why doesn't Richard just give him a chance? He's been working under him for two years, that's more than enough time to see that he's ready. After all, he graduated near the top of his class at Parsons. Well, sort of. And if Tilton's wealthy parents didn't donate so much money to the school, he most certainly would have been expelled.

Richard comes rushing into the office, frazzled, when he spots Tilton behind the desk. "What the hell are you doing?"

Tilton leaps. "Nothing. Sorry. You, ah, you wanted me? For something?"

Richard takes his rightful place behind the desk.

"Tilton. What kind of a name is Tilton?"

"It's from a town on Martha's Vineyard. Ever been? My parents own a place there. Um, a few places, actually."

"Really?" says Richard, unimpressed.

"Yes. My dad, I mean, my father runs a hedge fund," states Tilton proudly, almost bragging. Actually, he is

80

bragging. Richard could really care less and cuts him with a look.

"So, why are you working here? Or anywhere, for that matter."

"I've always wanted to be a designer. I know, if given the chance, I could be magnificent."

Richard frowns as he scans Tilton's ridiculous outfit up and down. He's overdressed, again, and over trying as always.

"Yeah, well. We all need to start somewhere, Tilton."

Tilton's shoulders drop with disappointment. Richard opens the desk drawer and removes a large sketch pad. "I need these sent to Brooklyn. We're delayed. Again."

Tilton takes the pad from Richard. "The subway is a nightmare to get to Brooklyn. I could get a bike messenger. Or maybe Uber."

"Seriously?" snaps Richard. "They needed to be there yesterday."

Out of options, he tosses the car keys.

"Any dents or even a tiny scratch on it, just keep driving. You understand?"

"Of course, Richard. I'll leave right away."

Richard watches Tilton scurry out. Maybe he should consider him for a promotion. He's not *that* bad a dresser. And he does try hard. Richard's been trusting him to drive his car. Well, it's not a *car* exactly - it's a Porsche. A Porsche 911 Turbo S Exclusive, to be exact. Maybe he should give the 'leetle chit' a chance.

He picks up the phone on his desk.

"Get me Michele in the human resources department, please."

BROOKLYN HOSPITAL

Shelagh sits comfortably at the front desk of The Brooklyn Hospital. She's perfectly content in her job as Hospital Admitting Clerk, but there's always been a hint of jealously and maybe some animosity between her and her cousin. Theresa just wanted it more, going to night school to get a nursing degree. Shelagh and her personality are better suited for people on this side of the curtain, as Theresa always reminds her. And Shelagh still gets to see Theresa and bust her balls about cleaning beds pans, wiping up puke and dealing with shit stained sheets - something she is kind enough to remind her loving cousin of daily.

She sees Theresa entering the Emergency Room,

"Have fun with the shit stains today, cuz," Shelagh jabs.

"Desk job is perfect for you, Shelagh," quips Theresa. "It hides your hips. You know you could never handle it back in the ER."

"Please. I'm tougher than you. It's science."

Theresa shoots her a puzzled look.

"I'm serious. Some university in Canada did a study that showed redheaded women can tolerate up to twenty five percent more pain than people with other hair colors."

"Reading a lot of Canadian medical studies, are ya?" asks Theresa dripping with sarcasm.

"I don't have the time or the crayons to explain it all to you brunette losers," replies Shelagh.

They both laugh hard.

"Listen, I'm gonna swing by later this week. My mother dug up a bunch of old pictures. She figured you'd want them."

"Great," says Theresa. "Thanks for the warning."

****

Theresa enters the emergency room to find a young girl in a soccer uniform sitting on the bed, holding her arm. Tears streak down her dirty freckled cheeks as her mother tenderly caresses her hair. In her nursing scrubs, Theresa looks softer, more caring.

"You know you're not supposed to use your hands in soccer, right?"

The girl forces a smile and wipes away another tear. "I know."

Theresa gives her a confident look, telling her she's in charge and everything is going to be OK.

"So, tell me Abby, did you win?"

Abby nods.

"Ok. You want the good news or the bad news?"

Abby's mother speaks up. "We'll take the bad news first."

"Well, the bad news is, no more soccer for a while."
She can see the tears begin to well up in Abby's eyes.
"Games. I mean no more soccer games. I'll talk to the doctor
and see if maybe you can practice. Slow jogs to keep your
foot work. Will that be OK?"

Abby wipes away a tear, leaving more streak marks on
her already dirty face. "What's the good news?"

"The good news is we have some pretty cool casts
that you can pick from," Theresa says cheerfully, selling the
idea. She opens a drawer showing off a vast selection of
colors for casts. Abby's mood changes a bit.

"I like the purple one."

"Good for you. For a minute there I thought you'd
pick the pink one. Pink is for little girls."

Theresa winks and begins to prepare the arm for
Abby's new purple cast.

"My parents are from Ireland," Theresa begins to tell
them. "They love soccer there, you know that? Only, they
call it fooball. Sorry, sweetie - does that hurt?"

"No. I'm OK."

"Of course you are. You look pretty tough. Bet the other girl cried when you knocked into her."

The mother speaks up. "It was a boy. Abby plays on the boys' team," she says in a tone that is not bragging, just stating fact.

"Good for you." Theresa leans in and whispers "Did *he* cry?"

Abby giggles. "I don't know. Maybe a little."

"You know, I broke my arm when I was your age. A boy did it. You have any brothers?"

"Matthew. He plays hockey."

"You two get along?"

"Sometimes."

The mother gives her a playful scowl.

"Not really," Abby admits.

Theresa continues to dress the arm and prepare the cast.

"My brother Richie and I were always fighting. One time, we were wrestling in the living room, and he fell on top of me. My mom rushed me to the hospital. She sat by my side, held my hand when they took me to X-rays. I was scared, not brave like you. My mother said that if I was really good, we could get ice cream."

Abby's mother gives Theresa a caring, tender smile. Theresa whispers so they both can hear.

"There's a Carvel about three blocks from here. Not that I go there or anything. I'm getting ready for Fashion week, ya know?"

She smirks and scans her own thick frame. Abby tries not to giggle.

Abby reminds Theresa of herself in many ways. As she places the arm into the cast, Theresa is thinking about Richie, and all the times they fought. And still do.

****

Tilton pulls Richard's shiny red Porsche into a dark alley, then slumps in the car quietly waiting, until he glimpses a figure in his rearview mirror. A short man approaches. Fashionably dressed. Funky blue-tinted glasses. Gleaming bald head with a neatly trimmed goatee, which makes him look angry. The obviously colored black hair on the sides of his head is squeezed into a teeny-tiny pony tail.

The driver side window slides down. A hand is extended with a sketch pad in its grasp. The man removes his glasses, puts them between his teeth and scans the design sketches.

Tilton clears his throat and asks nervously, "If you could hurry?"

The man scowls. "Marco Pacelli does not hurry."

"I...I really need to go," says Tilton timidly.

"These are the latest?"

"Yes."

The man's eyes widen with each sketch. "Remarkable. Simply remarkable."

He snaps a picture of each sketch with his cell phone as Tilton waits. They both look up and down the street.

A small, green bag is handed through the window. Tilton dabs a finger in and tastes the white powder. All good. He tosses the bag into the glove compartment, puts the gear in drive, and the Porsche peels out.

STATEN ISLAND

Fiona and Corey sit in her Prius. Jazz music on the stereo. Calm in the air.

"I should have taken Richmond," he says.

"Don't worry. We'll be fine."

"I just...I want to make a good impression," says a nervous Corey. "The school really needs this grant money."

Fiona rubs at her wrist. There's no rubber band fidget. She's with Corey, she thinks to herself, everything will be alright. She leans her head back and gives a weary smile of confidence.

"Have you checked?" he asks. "Anything yet?"

"No. I haven't had a chance," she replies. "I just got the kit the other day."

He gives her a look of concern.

"I'm fine, Dean Thompson. Really," she says in a reassuring tone.

"Don't jinx it, I'm not Dean yet. God, this light is taking forever."

Her head still leaning on the headrest, Fiona looks up at the red light, inhales, then blows a puff of air in it's direction.

"What are you doing?"

She smiles, more melancholy than happy. "My father used to do that. When the three of us were little, we'd sit at a red light and he'd say, 'Bet I can make this light turn green. Ready? One. Two. Three.' Whooosh. He'd blow a puff of air at the light, and it would turn from red to green. We all thought it was the coolest thing ever. Whenever we drove somewhere, we all hoped to hit the red lights so my Dad could do his thing."

Funny, she thinks to herself, how people seem to hate red lights. Especially her impatient sister.

"We didn't realize it because we were just kids, but my father was watching the other light, waiting for it to turn yellow so he knew exactly when to blow. We all thought he was magic."

She stares at the glowing red traffic light and begins to rub her wrist.

"We thought everything was magic back then. Or at least that's what we pretended."

BAY RIDGE

Michaleen sits on the front porch listening to his beloved Mets game on the radio. As a boy he loved all sport. Mostly traditional Irish games like Gaelic football, hurling, and soccer. He could never understand the American love of baseball. It was too slow, nobody hit anybody, and the manager wears a uniform. What's with tha'?

Once he moved to New York, he got used to listening to the games on the radio. His partner at the phone company, Jimmy Giglio, would have every game on as they drove all over Long Island stringing cable. Jimmy was a loud Italian, a great friend to Mick and a diehard Mets fan. The folks at New York Bell called them 'The Garlic and Gaelic Crew'. Jimmy Jigs, as Michaleen called him, lived and died by every pitch because he pretty much bet on every pitch. In fact, he bet on just about every part of the game. Who caught the next out. Was the next pitch going to be a ball? A strike? Will the pitcher scratch himself with his right hand or his left? Michaleen started to learn the cadence of the game - the pace, the lines, the over-under.

When he moved to Florida, he told everyone that Bridget wanted to get out of the cold New York winters. Truth was he needed to get the hell out of Brooklyn because he owed money to practically every bookie in the five boroughs.

Michaleen fiddles with something inside his Go bag when a police car pulls up. His eyes go wide. Shit! He instinctively slides the bag under him as the car door opens. WHEW! It's only Gerry.

"Gerry. How are ye, lad? No, ah, no beer on ye shoulder this time 'round?"

"No, Mick. Sorry."

"Shame, tha'. Theresa's not home yet. Come and sit. You can keep me company and listen to the Mets lose another game. Jaysus, they're playin' like shite. So, you come to ask for me daughter's hand in marriage, did ye? You'll make a handsome pair."

Gerry takes a seat on the top step. "I've asked her, you know. Three times, to be exact. She keeps saying, 'we'll see.'"

Michaleen scrunches his face. "We'll see. We'll see. That's the problem. It's the problem with all of them. They can't see. Starin' out the porthole, they are."

Gerry is once again lost on the fringes of the conversation. Michaleen sees the confusion on his face.

"I never told ye me boat story? Ah, we'll be needin' drinks. Ye...ye really didn't bring any beer?

"Sorry. No." Gerry is genuinely sorry. If Theresa had told him to stop by the liquor store on his way over, he would have gladly taken on that chore.

"It's alright. I got something in me Go bag - strictly for emergencies."

In an effort to help, Gerry reaches for the backpack, but Michaleen quickly grabs it away.

"No!"

"You OK, Mick?"

"Sure. Sure. Some of, ah...got some of Bridget's things in here, is all."

He removes a flask of whiskey from the backpack and pours into two cups. One for him. One for Gerry, painstakingly checking twice to make sure they're poured exact and even.

"Is Theresa really making you sleep on the porch?" asks Gerry.

"Makin' me?" Michaleen leans forward and scans the crisp clean sky. "A majestic view, isn't tha'? Can't see it from inside or down below."

A tink of cups as they toast and Michaleen begins to regale.

"Well, then. Now. I'll begin at the beginnin'. Me father's people were from Galway. Ballybane. He was a fisherman. Used to take me and me brothers to work the nets. First time I ever went out, was a fine soft spring morn'. Ocean was calm. Sky was blue. Once we got out beyond the breakers, the land got smaller, the ocean got bigger, the winds picked up and rocked the boat like the devil himself. Well, I was terrified. Ran below and hid me face. After a while the waters calmed down and they all yelled for me. Michaleen, come up. Come up and see it. But, I'd have none of it. Oh, every now and then I'd peak out the porthole, a small circle, too narrow to see anythin' at all. I spent the whole time down below, head in me lap."

He sips the whiskey and sits on the memory. "At dinner, they all talked of the things they'd seen. Dolphins off the port side. Sunset as it dipped into the ocean. That night, I lay in bed, sad and angry. Angry at meself. Me father comes in and sits on the edge of the bed. Michaleen, he says, you can't spend your life lookin' through the porthole. You gotta step out on deck so you can see the whole ocean."

Gerry is mesmerized, taking it all in.

"See lad, sometimes you gotta change yer view."

Theresa's car pulls down 89th Street and Michaleen sees it as his cue to leave. She'll probably be mad at him about something, he thinks, and he's not going to wait around to find out what or why.

Michaleen plops his hands on his knees, pushes himself up and proclaims, "I will arise and go now to Innisfree. And I shall have some peace there." Then performs his ritual. Keys. Teeth. Uh oh. No wallet.

"You, ah, you don't happen to have a twenty on ye by chance?"

"Huh? Oh. Sure." Gerry is more than happy to oblige.

In the laminated window of his wallet is a picture of his mother, Francine Mahoney. Not Theresa. Not his girlfriend of 12 years. Michaleen realizes in that moment he's not going to be a grandfather any time soon.

He takes the $20 with a wink, and he's gone.

****

On the other side of Brooklyn, Richard sits in a limousine at his own traffic light. Unlike Fiona, he's not thinking happy thoughts of family car trips and Michaleen making the light magically turn green. He's thinking of ways he's going to fucking kill that 'leetle chit' Tilton because Richard got a call from the warehouse over an hour ago that the sketches still haven't arrived.

The driver looks in the rearview mirror. "Sorry, Mr. Fitzgerald. Must be construction."

Richard impatiently peels back his sleeve to look at his Patek Phillipe.

"Do you want to me find another route?"

"Yes."

The look on Richard's face saying, Christ, what else could go wrong?

His cell phone rings.

"Tilton, where the hell have you been? So, we're all set? Fine." Click. No goodbye. No 'Thank you for delivering the sketches, Tilton.'

Richard is in no mood for excuses.

The driver is busy maneuvering the car through back streets.

"I know this seems out of the way, Mr. Fitzgerald, but it's what my phone says. You always gotta trust Waze."

Richard speaks up from the back.

"I don't need to go the warehouse anymore. Just take me back to Manhattan."

"We're not too far…"

"Turn down here. This street," says Richard.

"But Waze says…"

"Just do it. I know the area. Better than Waze, that's for sure."

The driver turns the car down a side street. Richard leans forward when his eye catches something out the window. He stares with a vague sense of unease.

"Stop the car."

"You sure Mr. Fitzgerald?"

He looks out the window again before committing, thinking to himself, this might be a mistake. "Yeah. I'm sure."

Richard opens the door and steps out.

****

Theresa gets out of the Chevy, beer and pizza in hand signaling its Saturday date night with Gerry. Mrs. Flanagan walks past with her dog Topper and gives a snarky greeting.

"Evening, Theresa."

"Hello, Mrs. Flanagan."

Neither of them actually wants to speak to the other. Rosemary Flanagan is the hands down GOAT (Greatest of All Time) for gossip, and Theresa doesn't want to hear any of the neighborhood intel.

"I was very sorry to hear about your mother, Theresa. She was a fine woman."

"Thank you," replies Theresa, trying to avoid eye contact or conversation because she can tell Mrs. Flanagan will want more information.

"I would have come to the service, but well," she gives a solid look of disgust. "No Christian Mass. Or even a burial. The thought of it."

"Those were my mother's wishes," says Theresa through gritted teeth.

"To be cremated? Is that right?" Mrs Flanagan asks coldly. "Odd. She never mentioned anything to me."

"You two talked a lot, did ya?" Theresa's tone trying to equal Mrs. Flanagan's air of disdain.

They didn't talk - at all. In fact, the consensus in the neighborhood was that if Rose Flanagan and Bridget Fitzgerald were ever left in the same room alone together, the world would turn so cold that all life as we know it would end.

Topper backs himself down, about to do his doggy business.

"Could you not let your dog...?"

But Mrs. Flanagan isn't listening.

"Well, your mother's with the saints now, God rest her, she'll finally have some peace. She certainly was a marvel of patience and endurance. We all know she had her share of crosses to bear. I mean, what with your father's carrying on and the lot."

Theresa is beginning to turn red, not agitated. Pissed. Really pissed. Mrs. Flanagan looks up and down the street and leans in as if she's sharing a secret with a close friend.

"And, well....her own child. In her own home. The shame of it."

YIPE! Topper suddenly yips in pain. Theresa stepped on his paw.

"Oh, my poor Topper!" Mrs Flanagan bends to pick him up. "Well...I never."

Theresa gets nose to nose. "Yeah. I know you never. That's your problem!"

For the first time, probably ever, Rose Flanagan is speechless. She walks away in a huff.

Pleased with herself, Theresa turns to head into the house...and steps in dog shit.

KELLY'S TAVERN

Michaleen sits surrounded by patrons at the bar. He's the life of the party wherever he goes, and even though he hasn't been at Kelly's for years, they all know that hanging out with him could end in a night in jail or a massive God-please-end-the-world-now kind of hangover.

The door opens, letting the sounds of the street stream in. The silhouette of a man stands in the doorway. Michaleen instinctively pushes the Go bag under his stool. It's not Gerry this time. To his surprise it's Richard.

"Richard, lad. And how'd you know I was here? "

"Call it a hunch."

"Gentlemen, say hello to my son Richard Fitzgerald, the famous designer of all things fashion."

Michaleen is genuinely happy to see him. In fact, he couldn't remember the last time he'd introduced his son to anyone.

The men at the bar all begin to check out their ill fitted attire - ugly mixtures of plaids and mismatched clothing. It's a fashion designer nightmare. Richard and Michaleen grab seats at the end of the bar as Mick begins to go through his ritual. Back pocket. Front pocket. Lips. Uh oh. Still no wallet.

"You, ah, you don't happen to…"

Richard pulls out his wallet, "I got it."

"Grand. Biffo, whiskey for me and my son."

Richard scans the bar up and down. "You don't happen to have any Macallan single malt, do you?"

Biffo looks with a scowl. "No. We don't *happen* to have that." He doesn't like Richard, or his kind - rich Millennials coming in from Williamsburg ordering IPAs and high-end bullshit.

"You don't come out to Brooklyn much do ya, son," observes Michaleen.

"Not if I don't have to," replies Richard, consulting his watch.

"Checking up on me then?"

"Fiona is worried you and Theresa might kill each other," Richard says only half kidding.

"We haven't. Not yet anyway," claims Mick as he reaches for the drink. "I never asked you kids to worry about me. In fact, I'd prefer you didn't."

Richard shakes his head and checks his watch - again.

"You keep looking at that thing like there's always somewhere else you gotta be."

"There is. Must be nice, Dad. No meetings. No deadlines. It's called responsibility."

"Spoken like a man who wears a watch and drinks Macallan single malt."

"It's a Patek Philippe. You don't even own a watch, do you?" asks Richard.

"Not even," says Michaleen proudly. "Tell me something. If I had a watch, would I be happy like you?"

"I'm happy," Richard shoots back.

Michaleen places his drink on the bar and turns to face his son.

"Your mother always had a keen sense for recognizing insincerity and half-truths, and had no patience for either. Me, I'm not so good at it. But I'm a betting man. And I'll wager that you're the most miserable man in this bar."

Richard looks around at the other men who have tuned in, with undisguised interest, to the conversation. He gets it.

He downs the whiskey in one shot, then grabs the bottle and pours himself another.

BAY RIDGE

Gerry cracks open a beer. He's always been comfortable in the Fitzgerald's house, especially their kitchen. The back door was always open, and the neighborhood kids would come and go. But God forbid if Mrs. Fitzgerald ever found out you didn't wipe your feet or slammed the back door.

It was there in that kitchen where Gerry got his first taste of Bridget's sharp tongue. She didn't save that just for her own children. Everyone was a potential target. One day Gerry made the almost fatal mistake of taking a second sleeve of Drakes coffee cake. *Gerald Mahoney, that's enough!*, she snapped, then proceeded to pat his expanding teenage belly, saying condescendingly, *And what are we to do about this?*

Theresa enters the kitchen, already a bit agitated. "Hey."

"Hey. How was your day?" asks the always cheerful Gerry.

"Do you have your gun with you?" she asks.

"What? Of course not. Why?"

Theresa wipes the dog shit from her shoe. "Bring it next time."

"You're in a good mood.," says Gerry handing her a beer. "Why do you let things bother you so much?"

Theres gives a sigh.

"I don't know. This should help," she says and plops a DVD onto the table. RIO GRANDE starring John Wayne and Maureen O'Hara. Gerry eagerly picks it up and reads the back cover.

"Nice. An hour and forty-five minutes. We should be alright."

"Alright for what?"

He knows he's about to walk out onto thin ice again.

"I gotta get back early. My mother said she wasn't feeling too good."

"It's bad enough she lives with you, now you can't even leave the house?"

Gerry feels the ice start to crack around him. "I don't think we should get into this right now. You're... emotional."

Oh boy. Here we go. Theresa is trying her best to contain her anger. She speaks in measured tones.

"But I'm not emotional, Gerry. That's the problem. I should be sad, right? You said so yourself."

"Ok. Calm down," he says coolly, trying to avoid completely falling into Theresa's icy black doom.

"I am calm. I'm relaxed. And I'm not sad. And I'm not angry. I'm just a fucking cow in a parking lot."

She lost him. A what? A frosty silence hangs over the room. She turns and braces herself at the sink, as if she needed support, and stares out the window, seeming more melancholy than angry.

"Do you know I broke my arm when I was ten? My mother thought I was exaggerating. '*You're fine,*' she said. '*You need to stop the rough-housing and act more like a lady. Maybe if you lost some weight you wouldn't hurt yourself from a simple fall.*'"

Theresa pauses, realizing the severity and hurt of sharing this sad truth aloud for the first time. Gerry doesn't know how to respond. Theresa continues.

"I had to wait for my father to come home so he'd take me to the hospital."

"I...I'm sorry," says Gerry as he steps towards her. But she pulls away angry and ashamed, still hiding behind her tough exterior. Theresa collects herself and states proudly,

"You know, I didn't even cry."

"I'm sure you didn't," Gerry says, more confirming her statement as a fact than consoling her.

Theresa collects herself and grabs the DVD. "Let's go watch the movie."

"I'm just trying to help," says Gerry.

He waits, knowing he's on the thinnest of thin ice, but decides to deliver the observation.

"You know, you can't blame all the problems in your life on your mother. Eventually you need to own it."

Goosh! Gerry falls through the ice, sinking slowly into the black void like Jack in the Titanic.

Theresa is speechless, which is reason enough for Gerry to be terrified. God damn it, Gerry was right, and that pisses her off even more. She doesn't know how to respond. The words are stuck in her throat until, fully flustered, she blurts, "Well...well...you slept with my cousin!"

"What?! What are you talking about?" pleads Gerry.

"Shelagh. She said you slept with her."

Gerry is incredulous. "That's not true. And you know it."

Theresa does know that's not true, she's just at her wits end and feeling cornered, so she punched back. Gerry spins off the ropes.

"She was being mean! You both were. God, you Fitzgeralds - you're all so good at that, aren't you?"

Theresa is taken aback by Gerry's newfound and sudden confidence. In all their years of dating, he's never so openly confronted her.

He's feeling empowered and liking it. "All due respect, but there you go. You know, growing up, everyone in the neighborhood looked up to you guys? My mother would say, why can't you kids be more like the Fitzgeralds? But it was all bull, wasn't it?"

He grabs his jacket and heads for the back door.

"Where are you going?"

"I don't know," he says over his shoulder, then stops before leaving. "I guess I'm just sick of looking at life through the porthole."

"Wait, what? What did you say?"

But he's gone.

And now Theresa is really pissed.

KELLY'S TAVERN

The empty glasses and slurred speech let everyone know that Richard and Michaleen have been at it for a while. Mick props his son up by the shoulders.

"Sit up, son. You're startin' to list slightly starboard."

He clunks the glass down loud enough to signal Biffo that he was in need of another. As he does, Richard looks closely at his father's hands - thick and calloused, littered with brown age spots, as if noticing them for the first time. It's the hands of someone who worked hard.

"You always smelled like fish," Richie slurs. "Growing up, I hated it."

Michaleen thinks long and hard before speaking.

"My father always smelled of the sea. He loved being a fisherman - said he was born for it. But it was tough, grueling work. Everything about it. You know, when people sit down at their fancy restaurants and order scrod and baked halibut, they're not thinking about the fishermen who wake up at 4:00 in the morning, cold and dark - ropes so cold they sting to the touch. They never see the callouses or the deep-creased scars on their hands from handling heavy fishing lines. They're just worried about what kind of wine goes with their meal."

Richard looks at his own soft, manicured hands. Michaleen looks at his son taking it all in, hoping the insight might resonate.

"Who you're from is as important as where you're from. I'm sorry if I let you down in that department."

"No. No. Sorry. It's not..." says Richard, feeling bad about his comments. He shakes his head and turns bitter.

"I'm just under so much pressure. Stockholders. Board members. Prepubescent teenage girls. They're all waiting on my next design. They all want me to be current and trendy."

"And what do you want to be, son?" asks Michaleen.

Richard thinks on that for a moment, then states almost dreamily, "I want to be timeless."

A sad, drunk smile forms as he looks at his father.

"You don't smell like fish anymore."

"I don't, huh?"

"No. You don't."

Richard leans over, a pronounced bend almost to the waist, and sniffs.

"You...you smell like dog shit."

Michaleen looks to the bottom of his shoe.

"That fuckin' dog. Biffo, you got any peanut butter back there in the kitchen?"

Biffo heads off in search of the request.

"What are you up to?" asks Richard.

His father looks him in the eye. "Let me ask you a question," Michaleen says with a mischievous smirk. "When was the last time you had any fun?"

Richard honestly can't remember.

MANHATTAN

Corey and Fiona gather for a rooftop deck dinner party. Strings of white lights illuminate the dinner table, soft music wafts over the Manhattan skyline. It's an older crowd, colleagues of Corey's from NYU, more polished, and academic. They see Fiona and begin to feign condolences. It's a bit overwhelming.

"I just heard about your mother, dear."

"I'm so sorry."

"Did you know Fiona's brother is Richard Fitzgerald?"

"I adore him."

"When is he releasing his new collection?"

"I'm dying to see it."

Fiona looks at Corey across the table. He smiles at her reassuringly with a look that says, '*Thank you for putting up with this for me.*' It's fine. It's important to Corey. She loves him. And he loves her.

Fiona looks around the table. Everyone seems to know what they're doing there except her, they're all comfortable in their own skin, absorbed in their environment.

Her eyes watch as a hand reaches across the table for the shaker of salt. Conversations are muted. She can only hear sounds, not words. She begins to rub at her wrist, looking anxious and uncomfortable and lost. Suddenly everything is in slow motion. BOOM. BOOM. BOOM. Each shake of salt hits her head like a drum.

Fiona closes her eyes. Her heartbeat begins to throb in her ears. Breathe, Fiona. Find your Zen. Think sunsets. Think puppies. Think a cow in a parking lot.

But it's no use. Her mind is elsewhere.

Ambulance lights flash. Neighbors out front watching as a stretcher is wheeled down steps. Bridget Fitzgerald standing at attention on the porch, a tightly coiled mixture of anger and embarrassment. The ambulance doors shut. Bridget glares, her face full of fury. She opens her mouth and begins to scream at a child standing by her side.

Fiona shakes the memory from her head. She's back at the dinner party, pale and confused. Everyone is staring. She pushes herself from the table and rushes out.

BROOKLYN

There's something about mornings in Brooklyn. Misty fog coming off the pavement. Sun streaming through the trees. A flight of birds etching themselves against the sky over the city. Michaleen always loved the quiet of early morning, it made him think of the days he spent on the boat with his father and brothers.

Christopher Fitzgerald considered it a virtue not to talk unnecessarily at sea and taught his sons the same. Sit. Smell the air. Listen to the ocean. Observe the world around you. No need to prattle on and on and ask 'morning questions.' Maybe that's where Fiona got her love for meditation. Relax. Just be. It was a family virtue rooted in the sea off Galway.

His morning quiet is interrupted as Theresa's Chevy Malibu pulls down the road. While Fiona was most certainly doing her daily yoga routine, and Richard was probably at some trendy CrossFit workout in Central Park, Theresa was on her way home from a graveyard shift at the hospital.

The car door squeals open and she makes her way up the steps to join her father. He has her cup of coffee prepared and ready to go, all set for her morning caffeine fix.

"Thanks," she says almost expecting he'd be there, and settles herself down on the top step.

They both respect the quiet and sit in silence. Theresa closes her eyes and cups the mug between her hands. This is kinda nice. Just me and Dad. Reminds her of the times when they were teenagers, running home to sit and catch the sunsets. Simpler times. Slower. When did everything change? They used to always sit out there. And then, they stopped. Bridget told them to *come in, the neighbors are watching.* Theresa remembers why now. She takes a long sip and moves her thoughts forward. She doesn't want to go there.

"You're looking especially smug this morning," she says, looking at a smirking Michaleen.

"Just enjoying the view, is all," he says with a shit-eatin' grin. "Wait for it."

They both look to the street. Coming down the sidewalk right on schedule is Rose Flanagan in her pale housecoat, stockings and slippers for her morning walk with Topper - only, the dog isn't really "walking" as much as Rose is sort of pulling him along.

"Come on, Topper," coaxes Rose. "What is wrong with you this morning?"

Nothing is wrong with Topper. In fact, the dog is just waking up from a deep night's slumber. But, something is off. Every few steps, the dog stops, plops himself to the ground and begins to lick his balls. Not just a casual lap, but a full on really-going-to-town-licking on those things.

"Somebody's certainly enjoying themselves this morning," yells Michaleen from the porch.

Rose Flanagan is dying from the embarrassment of her beloved dog Topper pleasuring himself along 89th Street for all the neighbors to see.

"Topper, stop that. Stop!"

But he just keeps licking away. Theresa tries not to laugh.

"What did you do to that dog?"

"Shame, tha', " says Michaleen. "Dog's getting more action than she is."

Theresa rolls her eyes and heads into the house as Michaleen continues to enjoy his morning coffee - and the view.

MANHATTAN

Ten miles away, across the East River, Richard stands on his patio watching the early morning city come to life below. He leans his elbows on the railing and stares down at the changing traffic lights along Columbus Avenue, illuminating the street with each changing hue of red, green and yellow. He takes a long sip of coffee and laughs to himself, tracing its source to the adventures with his father the night before. The whiskey and Guinness fog his memory a bit, but he's remembering bits and pieces. Jumping the fence and sneaking into Rose Flanagan's backyard. Coaxing Topper to come out through the dog flap on her back door. Crushing his Valium into powder. The dog licking it off his palm. The sight of his father smearing peanut butter all over Topper's, um, "puppy maker".

He busts a laugh and shakes his head. Jesus, that was fun. Michaleen was right. Richard honestly can't remember the last time he had fun.

Eduardo joins him and breaks his trance.

"Richard? Richard."

Richard continues to stare. "Did you ever notice the patterns?"

"You never stop working, do you," says Eduardo.

"I'm talking about the traffic lights. They're on a pattern. Each intersection in a row. Boom. Boom. Boom. Red to green to yellow. I always wanted to see how far I could get before they all went red. You know? Just hit the gas and fly down a Manhattan street. It would feel so…free."

He thinks on that, then leans over the railing and blows a puff of air in the direction of the lights. A sad, reminiscent smile forms on his face.

"Do you know what I wanted to be when I grew up?"

"A race car driver," Eduardo replies kiddingly.

"Close. A UPS driver."

Eduardo laughs. "I would love to see you in those ugly brown shirt and shorts."

"I like to think it's more 'russet-toned," quips Richard. "I always thought they were so cool. Drive big trucks. Park anywhere they want. Deliver packages and make people happy. Sort of like Santa Claus all dressed in... russet," they playfully say together.

Eduardo looks at him, concerned. He knows Richard is under a lot of pressure.

"Listen to me. You will be fine. This Marco Pacelli, he is nothing."

"It's not Pacelli. I don't know - maybe there is a curse. Sometimes I feel like the whole concept of happiness doesn't exist. It's just something peddled by our culture. A culture that I helped to create."

Eduardo takes the coffee from Richard and looks at him long and hard.

"My mother has four sons, I am the youngest. The baby. When she learned that I was gay, she cried. Mama, I ask her, why are you crying? I am still your baby. She looked at me - I don't cry because you are anything less. You will always be my baby boy. I cry because I fear your life will be more difficult than my other sons. And she was right. But, then I found you."

Richard finally smiles back.

"Look around, Richard. You have everything the world thinks makes you happy, but still...and you think you would find this happiness as a UPS Driver?"

After a beat, Richard agrees. "No, but I don't think dumping ashes from a plastic baggie is going to fix anything."

"Maybe not. But it's a start."

Eduardo joins him looking down at the pattern of street lights below.

"Everyone's family is fucked up, Richard. But yours? Tu familia esta algarete".

"What does that mean?"

"How do I say this? Your family is a real shit show."

Only, with his accent it comes out 'chit-chow.'

BROOKLYN

Theresa exits Word Bookstore and Stationery, a small independent community book shop on Franklin Street. It's the kind of place you can get lost in and no one, certainly no one Theresa hangs around with, would ever see her there.

Her arms full of recent purchases, she walks to the crosswalk and waits for the light. A car stops in front of her, mother and father in the front, two sisters and a brother fidgeting and teasing in the back. Theresa thinks how much they resemble her own family when they were that age, and it makes her smile. Maybe she should try some of that Fiona shit - happy, relaxed, Zen.

She makes eye contact with the little girl sitting by the window and gives her a friendly, caring smile. The girl shoots back a "Who the hell are you?" look and flips the finger. The light turns green, the car pulls away, and the rear tire sprays mud all over her shoes.

Fuckin' Karma.

She turns to leave and *slams* into someone, causing the books the spill all over the ground.

"Woah!"

"Sorry."

As she quickly bends to retrieve them, she hears, "I didn't think you could read." Awe, shit. Without even looking, she knows - it's Shelagh. "Those books must have a lot of pictures."

"Yeah, well...they were all out of Canadian studies on bitchy redheads," snaps Theresa, recovering the books. Shelagh bends to help, reading each title as she picks them up.

ANGER MANAGEMENT FOR DUMMIES.

MOTHERS WHO CAN'T LOVE: A Healing Guide for Daughters.

THE COW IN THE PARKING LOT: A Zen Approach to Overcoming Anger

Theresa tries to pivot. "They're Fiona's. You know her. Incense. Candles. John Tesh music and shit."

Shelagh knows she's lying. Cousins know. In many ways, they are closer than sisters. Closer in age than Theresa and Fiona, and certainly in demeanor. Shelagh changes the subject on purpose.

"I heard about you and Gerry."

"Yeah, well...we're working through some issues."

Theresa is still flustered.

"Mind if I have a go at him then?" asks Shelagh.

"I thought you already did. You said he sucked in bed."

"Oh, right. He did, didn't he."

They both laugh.

"Too early for a drink?" asks Shelagh.

"Never."

****

Brooklyn is littered with trendy outdoor cafes. While Shelagh and Theresa have lived through and hated the gentrification of their neighborhoods, they've both been fortunate enough to watch their real estate values triple since they each took over their parents' properties. But to take advantage of the market, that would mean they'd have to sell. And where the hell would they move to? Williamsburg? Ugh, they hate Millennials almost as much as Biffo does. A condo in Florida? Bridget and Michaleen tried that, and they both know how that worked out. Bay Ridge born. Bay Ridge bred. Bay Ridge forever.

They sit and enjoy the scenery as the colorful people of the neighborhood pass by; men with overgrown beards, fedora hats and body tattoos; women with purple hair, nose rings and ear gauges. This is not the Brooklyn that Shelagh and Theresa grew up in.

"Richie really needs to open a store down here," says Shelagh.

"You think? He still has a bunch of his old clothes at the house. Maybe I should have a yard sale. List them as 'Original Designs by Fitzy.' These people love all that retro shit." They laugh over pint glasses of beer. Its' only 11:00 a.m.

"Here," says Shelagh opening a large folder and spilling pictures onto the table. "I was on the way to your house when you bowled me over in the street. My mother thought you might want these."

Theresa begins to sift through the assortment of old black and white photos and Polaroids. Bridget with her sisters Eleanor and Martha. The Fitzgerald and Murphy kids together. She's probably not far from Theresa's age and has an eerie resemblance to Fiona.

Theresa flips through each picture as if looking at a total stranger. Her mother is beautiful. In one photo, Bridget is wearing a paper hat on her head, laughing so hard and acting…no, it can't be. Theresa looks closer. Yes. Bridget Fitzgerald looks like she's acting silly. It's a word and mood that Bridget would never stand for in her own children. Sitting there staring at the photos, it was hard for Theresa to ever imagine her mother as young. And silly. And happy.

"I've never seen these."

"Look at this one," says Shelagh handing over a Polaroid. "That's you and me at your 13th birthday."

Everyone is at the kitchen table. Eating. Laughing. In the background, Bridget is standing at the sink, alone, cleaning dirty dishes. At the time, it surely went unnoticed. It always did, Bridget wandering around the edges of a party, getting people's dishes, removing full ashtrays of cigarettes, making sure glasses and bottles were properly set on coasters so they wouldn't leave water rings on her furniture. No one ever thought about who organized everything, spending hours cleaning, setting the table, cooking pot roast in ninety-degree heat in a kitchen so small it barely held five people, let alone the twenty or more that Michaleen would invite from Kelly's for every occasion. The kids would all be showered and dressed in their Sunday best, clothes ironed and laid out on the beds the morning of the party, any rips sewn and repaired the night before. The next morning everyone would wake up and the kitchen would be magically back in order, any leftover food neatly put away in Tupperware containers. *There's no reason to throw away good food.* Breakfast would be ready, and everyone was back to their daily routines.

Something about the picture hits Theresa. Maybe it's the non-descriptive, simple task of doing nothing spectacular, cleaning dishes, while everyone around her is having fun.

"I don't remember my mother ever laughing or having fun or, God forgive, acting silly. She was always too busy doing something - I thought to avoid it."

Theresa thinks for a moment before speaking.

"When I was a teenager, I'd wished her dead hundreds of times a day. I imagined the world would be a better place with her gone. But, things are pretty much the same... just one less person to blame everything on." Gerry's words still sting.

Shelagh looks at her cousin and can see that she is hurting. "So, how you doin', Tree? You OK? You wanna talk about this Book of the Month Club thing you got going on, over here?" she asks with the perfect mixture of true concern and sarcasm.

"I'm fine," says Theresa back. But she's not.

Silence. Shelagh knows what her Aunt Bridget was like.

"Did I ever tell you I used to hate coming over your house for holidays?" says Shelagh.

"Really? Why?"

"Ah, I'd have to listen to your mother brag on and on about you three."

"My mother? Cut the shit."

"I'm serious. Then the whole way home my mother would be all pissed off. 'Why can't you be more like your cousin?'"

Theresa laughs.

"I never told you any of this?" says Shelagh, and does her best Bridget imitation. "*Did ye hear Theresa made the Honor Roll? Did ya hear Theresa is on the varsity softball team. And she's only a freshman.*"

"Now I know you're lying. She never even came to a game."

Shelagh waits, letting it settle in a bit.

"You know our family. We never show emotion. Ever. Do you remember the time your Mom came to the ER? She thought she broke her wrist? I'm sitting with her while you're running all over the place. Cleaning bedpans. Wiping puke. You know, the typical bullshit you do back there behind the curtain."

"You know you couldn't handle it."

Shelagh laughs. "No. Your mother was watching you the whole time. Helping patients. Sitting with kids. Walking elderly to the bathroom. 'Look at my Theresa', she says. And she looks off, almost sad, ya know? 'The way she is with people...so patient and kind. Makes me almost - ashamed, the way I act sometimes.'"

Theresa is taken aback and takes a long sip of her beer.

"Now," says Shelagh in a dramatic tone, "I'm gonna give you some advice. Stop being a dickhead."

"Words to live by," deadpans Theresa.

"You know what I mean. You wanna end up like me?"

She points to her bag of groceries. Cat food. Annie's Mac and Cheese, single serving. A sad DVD movie. "Go. Talk to Gerry. Or else I *will* bang him - and good. And then he'll never want you back."

They share a smile and heartfelt hug.

STATEN ISLAND

There had always been an ebb and flow to Fiona's moods - whole weeks, even months where she'd be, or at least seem to be, at peace. Then, for no apparent reason she'd be crippled with anxiety. Fiona could feel the sea of change as it swelled up inside her. Most of the time it was the result of something to do with her family. A phone call. Stumbling upon an old photo. A trip to Bay Ridge to pick something up. Small sounds would startle her. Her eyes would float back and forth, her breathing labored and her chest tight.

When Corey asked what was wrong, she would usually try to change the subject and just twist at the rubber band on her wrist. They've been through this before, but last night was a particularly bad episode.

Fiona lies curled up in their rumpled bed looking tired and frail as Corey brings over a cup of herbal tea and sits beside her.

"I'm so sorry about last night."

"You don't need to apologize, Fi."

"I know it may seem irrational to you, but...I never know when it's going to hit."

Corey throws a leg up on the bed and twists to look her in the eye. "I just wish, maybe if I saw it coming, I could help."

"It doesn't have 'a look', Corey. I don't need to be trembling or hyperventilating to be anxious. Most of the time you won't know it unless I tell you."

She puts the tea down on the nightstand, too upset to drink. It's a complicated thing, and it's frustrating her more and more.

"Maybe the stress of all this is too much," says Corey in an effort to calm her. "Your mom passing away. My new job. Donald Trump is President! I mean, what kind of a world would we be bringing a child into?"

They never talked about getting married, it was always just assumed that they would live together, forever. Corey's belief system, as it were, was very progressive. Theirs would be a more spiritual union, and unlike Gerry, Fiona was perfectly happy to never actually go through a formal proposal, the engagement process and a full-blown wedding ceremony.

So, when the discussion of having children came up with Corey a few months ago, it really took Fiona by surprise. Maybe they should.

"Even when things are wonderful, I'm waiting for something horrible to happen. It feels like I'm drowning all the time," she says as the tears begin to well in her eyes. Corey takes her hand, trying to think of the right thing to say.

"You know, Fi, it's easy to drown when you're trying to be everyone else's anchor."

She gets it. Being the family peacemaker takes its toll.

"Here. Drink your tea. It always helps."

She takes it from him and slides deeper under the covers.

"Do you want your pills?"

She nods yes.

The nightstand drawer slides open. Among the pill bottles, meditation pamphlets and calming beads are two items that may be the deepest cause for Fiona's recent anxieties - an unopened Early Pregnancy Test, and the yellow baggie of ashes.

"What is this doing in here?" asks Corey grabbing the bag from the nightstand drawer.

"I didn't think it was fair to have you look at it every day."

Corey is a bit miffed by its presence. "I thought we talked about this. If your brother and sister won't do it, you still need to. It's part of your healing process."

"We said we'd do it together. Besides, it's...it's just table salt," she says, trying to lighten the mood.

"It's what it represents, Fiona. An act that releases you from your mother's orbit. Letting go may finally set you free."

Her mother's orbit. If it was only that easy, they would have all dumped the bags into the kitchen sink the morning their father gave them out with instructions. But that's not the way it's supposed to be done.

Curse or no curse, they would all have to do this together.

MANHATTAN

In his rush to get back in a timely and accident-free manner, Tilton forgot that he left the green plastic bag in Richard's car. He rushes through the parking garage, his heart pounding in panic. He approaches the Porsche, cups his hands and peers through the passenger side window. Shit! What the hell is he going to do?

BOOP BOOP. Suddenly, the car lights flash. He looks up, startled to see Richard standing on the other side with his key fob, unlocking the car.

"Tilton. What are you doing?"

Tilton is in heart attack mode and keeps glancing toward the glove compartment.

"Richard. Hi, ah. I think I may have left…" but he catches himself. "Nothing. I just, I wanted to see…um, have you ever been to Martha's Vineyard?

"What?"

"You could stay at my parents place if you ever want to."

"You mean, like, a sleep over party?" says Richard with biting sarcasm.

"No. It's just…well, you could use the house whenever…it's pretty big, and…"

But Richard is unimpressed. He opens the car door trying to move on.

"I'm more of a Hamptons man."

"Yes. Of course." Tilton is in full blown panic mode, trying to distract. "How...how are your new sketches coming along? You know, for the Fall collection."

"Fine."

"I was thinking...I've been working here for a couple years now, and, maybe I could start working on the design team."

"It's not a good time," says Richard over the rev of the engine. Tilton taps on the passenger window, still trying to get his attention.

"Well, when then?"

"You're not ready."

"I am ready," says Tilton, a bit more forceful than he wanted. "I'm ready now."

Richard is in no mood for this. He scans Tilton's outfit up and down and condescendingly replies.

"No. You're not."

"Maybe I should just go work for Marco Pacelli," states Tilton, brimming with cockiness. Richard is stung. He pushes the button and slowly, agonizingly, rolls the passenger window down.

"What? What did you say?"

"I'm just saying. If you don't see my talent, maybe someone else will."

Richard takes a deep breath, at first angry, but then stops himself. He looks at Tilton making a stand. Good for him, the 'leetle chit'. Richard turns off the engine, loosens his grip on the steering wheel and softens.

"Look, I understand your frustration. You're a good kid, and you've been a dedicated employee. You have drive, energy, ambition."

Richard stops and reflects for a second. He's on unchartered territory here, trying to be compassionate and listening.

"I'm sorry if I don't tell you that enough, Tilton. We're not...I'm not very good at expressing my feelings sometimes."

Tilton is taken aback by Richard's sudden openness. "I asked Human Resource to bring me your file to review."

After a moment, he says, "We'll see."

He sounds just like Theresa.

"Thank you, Richard. I...I appreciate that." He really doesn't know what to say.

"Have a good night."

Richard fires up the engine and backs out, leaving a somewhat stunned Tilton just standing there.

Tilton suddenly remembers what he came to the garage for in the first place. Shit.

He watches the Porsche drive away and whispers to himself, "Fuck me."

Richard glances back at him through the rear-view mirror and whispers to himself, "Fuck you."

BAY RIDGE

As a general rule, if the phone rings after 10:00 at night someone is sick or in the hospital. If someone knocks on your door after midnight, then it's official - someone is dead. Gerry runs through the living room in his sweat pants, NYPD T-shirt, oversized bathrobe and clicks on the porch light to see Theresa standing in the doorway.

"What the...Theresa? Is everything OK? What time is it? Jeeze, must be two in the morning." Even with the terror of a post-midnight door knock and his heart racing, Gerry still doesn't swear.

Theresa responds in a calm and matter of fact manner.

"I've been thinking, Gerry. And, well, the answer is yes."

Gerry is still trying to get his rapid heartbeat down. "Yes, everything is OK?

"No. Yes. I mean, yeah, everything is OK. I'm saying yes to your other question."

"About what time it is?" he's half asleep too.

"No, Gerry. Jesus, you're not making this easy. You want me to do this thing? Ok, I gotta do it. I'm gonna do it," she says convincing herself and laboring to get down on one knee.

"Well, here I am, Gerry. Down on one knee. Not even sure I can get back up. But, what I want to say is…"

She pauses, the words stuck in the back of her throat.

"What I *need* to say is, I…I love you. Yeah. There. I said it. I love you, Gerry."

He's taken aback. "You do?"

"Yes. Of course, I do. Now help me up, will you for Chrissake?"

He takes her arm as she struggles to her feet, anxious and relieved.

"Whew. That felt pretty good," she says. And it did, too.

"Thanks," says the ever polite Gerry

"Thanks? That's your response? Thanks?"

"Well, what do you want me to say?"

"I don't know. I…I guess I thought you'd say it back."

"I have said it, Theresa. I've said it for twelve years."

They both stand there, surveying the situation. She's not sure where to go from here. Like her brother, we are officially on unchartered emotional territory.

She states softly, convincing herself as much as confessing to Gerry.

"I just...I didn't want to follow my parents' miserable version of marriage, ya know? And... I figured you have to like yourself before you can commit to another person, and, well, I haven't liked myself for a really long time."

He thinks. She waits. It seems like an eternity. She musters the courage.

"Gerry, will you marry me?"

Maybe it's the suddenness of the late/early hour awakening, or the fact that he's so caught off guard, but he just can't look her in the eye.

"Theresa. I...I..." but there's confusion and trepidation in his voice. Not like this. Not this way.

His cell phone rings. (It's in his robe, never far from his person.) Speed dial #1. It's his mother calling from upstairs.

"Everything's fine, Ma. Yes, go back to bed. I know it's late. Ok, Ok, I'll be right there."

He turns back to Theresa. "I better go. Sorry."

The door closes, and Theresa stands there - devastated and alone.

MANHATTAN

Richard revs the engine of his Porsche as he waits at the light, the streets eerily quiet. He inhales a deep breath and blows in the direction of the red traffic light.

Like dominos, each intersection starts to change in succession red to green. Boom. Boom. Boom. A smirk forms. His designer shoe presses on the clutch. His manicured hand shifts into gear. He hits the gas and tires squeal, violently thrusting his head into the leather seat as the car flies through each intersection.

The glow of green lights bounces off the window's reflection, and he smiles wide. So, this, he thought, was what it feels like to be his father. Reckless. Out of control. Happy. Free.

STATEN ISLAND

A pale and nervous Fiona grips the steering wheel of her Prius as she sits waiting at her own red traffic light. Corey is in the passenger seat, ready to coach her on.

"I don't know about this Corey," she says nervously.

"You can do it, Fi."

"It's so late. Or early. Why are we doing this?"

"This is good, though. There won't be as many cars on the road. Just take it slow. Remember the strategies we worked on. Breathe. You'll be fine."

He looks aside at the opposing light.

"Ok. Almost. You ready? Do it with me. One. Two. Three."

Fiona reluctantly joins in, and together they blow a puff of air towards the signal. The light turns green and Fiona starts to drive up the ramp onto the Bayonne Bridge.

"Baby steps, Fi. Don't worry. This bridge is only, like, five thousand feet. You got this."

"Five thousand!?" she yells, terrified.

"Just focus on the road. Try some Ujjayi breathing. In and out. In and out. Find your Zen stillness."

She's in full blown panic mode. "I can't do this."

"You'll be fine," he encourages. "Think sunsets and puppies."

"Fuck puppies!"

He stifles a laugh. "OK. OK. Talk to me. Tell me a story."

She keeps driving, slowly, terrified, as random cars whiz past her slow-moving Prius.

"What? What story?"

"I don't know," he pleads. "Tell me the one about your father and the lights."

"My Chakra is all out of alignment. I've lost my Chi."

She slams her hands on the wheel. "We gotta get rid of those fuckin' ashes!"

Corey is doing his best to calm her down. "You're doing great, Fiona. Just focus."

Just be, Fiona tells herself. Get out of your head. In through the nose, out through the mouth. Finally, she blurts out, "Peppermint Patty!"

"What?"

"York Peppermint Pattys. That was my mother's favorite candy."

Corey smiles. Fiona is focused and intense and doesn't take her eyes off the road.

"She'd keep them in the back of the fridge, hidden away from everyone. She…she liked them cold."

Fiona is getting better, more comfortable. Corey encourages her to go on.

"We could open one present on Christmas Eve from each other. That was it. Then we'd have to wait to open the rest in the morning."

"Sounds reasonable. What was her favorite time of day?"

"Late afternoons. Summertime." Fiona is starting to get a bit more relaxed. She breathes in and out. "Everyone would be lighting their grills. The whole neighborhood smelled like charcoal fluid. We'd all be outside - me, Richie and Theresa – would run home so we could sit on the porch and watch the sunset with Dad. The sky would fill with color and it would wash all over the street and the houses."

Two hands firmly on the wheel and eyes straight ahead, she is strong. Confident.

Corey looks at her proudly and says, "Sounds like magic."

Cars continue buzz by, some honk their horns, but fuck them - she's driving over the God damn bridge.

KELLY'S TAVERN

Michaleen is at his usual bar, in his usual seat with a half-finished Guinness in front of him. Biffo stands sentry, cleaning glasses with a rag.

"Don't forget to pay your tab, there Mick."

"Do I ever?" shoots Michaleen, shocked at the accusation.

"Yes."

"Well, I won't today."

He begins to pat himself down. Keys. Teeth. Uh oh. No wallet. Biffo has seen this act before, and he's not about to fall for the 'I left me wallet in my other pants' routine.

A woman is reading at the other end of the bar. Attractive. Unassuming. Clearly well off by her clothes and demeanor. She's older than Mick, but not by too much. She motions for Biffo and slides a $20 in his direction, indicating that she'll pay the tab. Things like this always seem to work out for Michaleen.

"Happy now?" he mugs.

"Never been happier," says Biffo as he opens the register.

"And make sure you give the woman her exact change…ya big ignorant fuck from Offaly."

The bar erupts in laughter. Now they know the origin of the nickname. Biffo has three solid inches and a good twelve to fifteen pounds on Michaleen, but he's been around long enough to know that Mick was a Golden Gloves boxer back in the day (hence the reason for a few missing teeth), and that despite having his ribs broken twice, replaced a hip, bursitis in his shoulder, and the need for glasses to see anything closer than four feet, on his worst day Michaleen could still beat the hell out of anyone in the place.

Michaleen approaches the woman and looks back to the stool where he was sitting.

"And how's the view from this side of the bar?"

"The view?" she asks.

"Musta' thought I was Brad Pitt from this angle."

She smiles, and he takes a seat beside her.

"What's a lovely young thing like you doin' in this motley establishment?"

"Just stopped in for a drink. I'm Caitlin. From Bensonhurst."

"Caitlin? What's a Caitlin doing in Bensonhurst? Place is chock full of Italians - the state of it. They may have built the houses in Brooklyn, but the Irish built the bridges and the tunnels that got them here."

Caitlin can't resist the impish smile and piercing blue eyes.

"I'm actually moving to Breezy Point," she says. "I have a boat there."

Michaleen's eye's go wide.

"Biffo. We'll be needin' drinks over here, if you please."

He leans in close. "I'm a bit of a fisherman me self."

"Really," she says, her demeanor full of flirtation. "Well, isn't that convenient. It's not really a boat - actually, it's more of a yacht."

"And what's the difference?" asks Mick.

"You can fit a boat on a yacht," she says with a slight cough. "Excuse me. I've had a bit of a tickle lately."

Michaleen is officially in love. He turns to Biffo.

"Leave the bottle."

He pours – painstakingly checking twice, making sure they're poured exact and even.

"Well, then. Now. I'll begin at the beginnin'. Me father was a fisherman from Ballybane, near Galway - used to take me and me brothers to work the nets..."

Caitlin listens intently as Michaleen tells his boat story, falling for him with each word.

BAY RIDGE

The Irish do death well. The wake at home, the
funeral mass, the long gathering at the local pub, the
memorial mass a month later and the anniversary mass every
year thereafter. Nope. Not Bridget Fitzgerald. She would
have none of that. Far be it for Bridget Fitzgerald to be
unprepared. She had every detail planned. Someone will sing.
But not Danny Boy, it's too long, too sad and far too Irish.
There's to be no photo in the program, she was never happy
with any picture ever taken of herself. A quiet death, an
abrupt cremation, a small service, and a cold brass urn
complete with a handy dandy set of instructions.

Theresa thinks of all that planning as she sits at her
kitchen table twirling the plastic red baggie in her hand,
slowly coming to the realization that she may have lost Gerry,
her father may never leave, and she still has to dump a third
of her mother's ashes somewhere. In fact, she hasn't even
opened the envelope to find out where.

The back-door knob jiggles. Can't be Gerry, can it?
He'd never come at this late an hour. Someone is trying to get
in, only they are pushing the door when it needs to be pulled.
After a few unsuccessful attempts, she can see that it's
Michaleen, tipsy from his night at Kelly's. He shuffles in
thinking he's been super quiet, when in fact half the

neighborhood could hear his comedic struggle with the door. He jumps when he sees Theresa sitting alone in the dark.

"Jaysus, ye gave me a start."

"You're a real piece of work, you know that?" says Theresa.

"I've been told that, yeah. No date night tonight?"

"Nope. Thanks to your boat stories, I think Gerry jumped ship."

"You're agitated," says Mick.

"Jesus, I hate that word. I'm beyond agitated. I'm full blown pissed off."

She is. You can almost see steam coming off her head.

"Jaysus," says Michaleen. "You sound like yer mother."

Her eyes shoot daggers. "There's still room in that jar, old man."

His twinkling blue eyes won't get him out of this one.

"We'll be needin' drinks," he says and reaches for the whiskey above the fridge.

"Forget it. Richie and I polished it off the other night."

"And ye didn't replace it? Did I not teach you kids any manners?" he says swinging the ever-present backpack off his shoulder. "Lucky for you, I keep a spare in me Go bag. Strictly for emergencies."

Michaleen pours into two coffee mugs, painstakingly checking twice, to make sure they're exact and even. They both sit for a while, cautious, weighing words, the red baggie of ashes between them. Theresa breaks the silence.

"Do you know she never told me she loved me?"

"Wasn't their way. None of them, that Murphy clan. As cold a lot as you'll ever find. You never met her father, your Grandfather, John Murphy."

"Mom never talked about him. She never said anything about her past. Like it didn't exist."

"Your mother was far too proud, or embarrassed."

Theresa looks at her father for answers.

"I met him on a few occasions, and they were never pleasant. John Murphy didn't talk so much as growl. Ooh, his drunken rants were epic - all aimed at Bridget, Eleanor and Martha. He was a tough one, tha'. The man could dismantle an emotion or deflate an ego with a single word."

Sounds familiar, thinks Theresa.

Michaleen can see his daughter is hurting, so he shifts gears.

"I decided long ago to abstain from most general forms of regret, it'll only eat away at your hull, but...." Michaleen swirls the brown liquor in his coffee mug.

"I know I had a lot to do with your mother's disposition. I'm not proud of many of the things I did. And, I think, maybe she was tough on you kids because of me."

"That doesn't make it right," she says, sadly stating fact.

"No...no, it doesn't," he nods, pondering the right next words. He looks his daughter in the eyes because this part is important. "But, I think your mother never gave love, because she never properly received it."

The words sit out there, float around for a bit, then settle on Theresa. She picks up the plastic red baggie, inspecting it closely as it dangles between her fingers.

"She sure has us three pegged, huh? Red. Green. Yellow. I'm the angry one. Richie is materialistic. And Fiona...well, Fiona is terrified."

"You're wrong, Theresa. You're not seein' things clear."

Theresa gives a sad, knowing smile. "I know. Change the view, right? Step out on deck."

Michaleen spots the collection of self-help books sitting on the counter.

"What yer lookin for...you're not gonna find in those books."

"And you're not gonna find it in that bottle," she replies. She got him, and he knows it.

"Fair enough. Fair enough."

Michaleen plops his hands on his knees, pushes himself up and proclaims. "I will arise and go now to Innisfree. And I shall have some peace there."

Items slide across the worn Formica table top. Keys. Wallet. A plastic container for teeth.

"Good night, Dad."

Michaleen kisses his daughter lovingly on top of the head.

"Good night, love."

He leaves her alone with her thoughts - and her mother.

JOHN MURPHY

John Murphy raised his family in St Mary's Park in central Limerick, one of the most disadvantaged areas of Ireland - abandoned, as he would say, by state agencies for decades. It was an excuse he used for never being properly employed. Bridget and her sisters grew up among a crumbling collection of run-down, knocked-down, boarded-up dwellings dotted along a misery of cratered roads. Eleanor would tell Shelagh stories where *"rats would be coming into the house and they'd nearly sit down and talk to you."*

John was a stoic man with an angry disposition and iron fist. The girls lived in a constant shadow of fear, as did their mother Anne. Growing up, Bridget had no fond memories of a happy, tender, or even sober father. The oldest of the three, Bridget tried to shelter her sisters Eleanor and Martha from their father's drunken rants, all aimed at their plainness and lack of prospects for a man. Unflagging in his Christian beliefs, John used the term 'spare the rod and spoil the child' not only as a motto, but a habit. Under his strict parenting, excitement or happiness would simply dry up and

155

blow away, as did any feelings of hope and contentment. They lived amid the absence of affection. Bridget Fitzgerald learned from the best, a disposition passed along from father to daughter.

As the girls became teenagers, John Murphy would drill them on abstaining from any type of *'male-female physical connections.'* Boys would never come around out of fear - fear of the neighborhood, fear of what the girls may do once they were released from his grasp and fear of John Murphy.

The people from St Mary's Park were marked as *fecking messers*, the Irish slang for a sloppy or troubled person. While other immigrants talked dreamily of home and their youthful carefree days in Ireland, Bridget would find those moments as her cue to leave the conversation or change the subject. She spent her adult life with either a chip on her shoulder or anger in her heart, constantly trying to hide from her past.

When Bridget had an opportunity to leave Ireland for America and re-invent herself, she jumped at the chance. She found a sponsor, took every cent she had saved from doing laundry in the nearby hospital, and she took off for America, the land of freedom.

Being from St Mary's Park wasn't the only secret that Bridget would hold.

It was there, one summer night at Kelly's Tavern that she saw him. Michaleen Christopher O'Connor Fitzgerald. Gameslayer. Ladies' man. Outlaw. Golden Gloves boxer. Regaler of tales. She'd seen him there on a few occasions, always the life of the bar. Everyone loved him. And, she thought, maybe she did too. At least that night, she could.

What could be more foolish, she thought, than staking your life on a scandalous whim - one capricious fling of clumsy nakedness and reckless bumping in the back of a New York Bell phone company van. All those years of repressed Catholic school sexuality and John Murphy's degrading comments for a momentary obliteration of thought and guilt and conscience. Maybe that's why she was so quick to give up the one thing she thought she could control - her virginity.

So, she gave herself to him, a man she knew had the power to destroy her, through carelessness, or misguided foolish intention - and in that moment, on that night she didn't care. She was reckless. Out of control. Free.

She knew almost immediately, there was something about it that whispered in the back of her mind. But it wasn't until weeks later that she scientifically confirmed the fact. Being raised in a country and a religion that did not allow, or even say the word, abortion, Bridget did the right thing. The

157

Christian thing. And in this patch of pain and regret, the angry seed was born, subconsciously blaming Michaleen, then the children, and harboring until death a secret she found shameful enough to keep to herself for years. Theresa was the accident. Richie, drunken forcefulness. But Fiona...baby Fiona. She was one night when Bridget conceded and felt something, needed something, after years of raising two small children.

Was it a selfish act again? A way to feel reckless like her husband? Maybe. And maybe that's why Bridget was sometimes softer on Fiona than the other two. Sometimes. Most of the time she was creating a triangle of problems between siblings, pitting one against the other, each taking a turn in her crosshairs.

And that was that. No more. No '*male-female physical connections.*' "A man's got needs," Michaleeen would say. So he had to look elsewhere - and she knew it. Bridget's focus was to be on motherhood. She had a job to be done, serious work with serious repercussions. Raise a strong well-grounded Christian family. Mannered, loving and happy. Or at least keep up that appearance.

You would think having the children would have made her happy - but it only made her more resentful.

It was three more people in the world who would grow up to not love her properly.

MANHATTAN

Police lights flash behind a shiny red Porsche. An officer taps on the glass as Richard sheepishly rolls the window down.

"Evening, officer."

"License and registration please."

Richard scans the officer's jacket.

"You know you should just use one button. It slims the silo…"

The officer cuts him off. "License and registration."

"Yes. Of course," says Richard as he reaches across the seat and pops open the glove compartment. Their eyes go wide. Richard has a 'How the hell did that get in there?' look.

"Step out of the car please, sir."

"I...I think I can explain."

"Out of the car. Now."

The officer reaches into the glove compartment and retrieves a small plastic green baggie.

"This is a huge misunderstanding," pleads Richard.

"You see, actually, I'm pretty sure that's my…"

A stern look tells Richard to shut up. The officer dabs a finger into the baggie and tests a sample on his tongue.

"Oh, my God. Stop!" screams Richard. "That's my mother!"

The officer spins Richard and slaps handcuffs on his wrists.

"Really? She must be from Columbia."

"Actually," says Richard, his cheek pressed against the hood, "she's from Ireland."

****

Richard's designer outfit and leather Testoni shoes make him stand out among the drunks, bums and petty thieves in this late night 24th Precinct round up. He scans the other inmates clothing, about to offer advice when someone yells. "Fitzgerald! Let's go. You made bail."

Theresa is there waiting for him. He stops, thinking for a moment he might be better off back in the holding cell.

"How'd you know I was here?"

"Gerry's Captain called me. He figured you'd want to keep this quiet. Jesus, Richie. Cocaine?!"

"It's not mine."

"Right. Then whose is it?"

"I have no idea, but it's in a green bag, like the one Dad gave me."

Suspicion is on both their minds.

"Come on, Richie. Dad is a lot of things. Drinker. Serial adulterer. But a drug dealer?"

"Then how did it get into my car?" He stops and thinks on it some more. "Could you call Gerry? I really need to keep this quiet. At least until I get it all figured out."

"Yeah, well, me and Gerry aren't really on speaking terms right now."

"Why? What happened?"

"Nothing. It's just not a good time to…"

"Please, Theresa. If my distributors hear about this. Or the shareholders. Or my customers."

"Of course. Fitzgerald's. Gotta keep up appearances," she says with a bite of truth.

"Theresa," he pleads. "Please."

She looks at her brother, desperate for help, and dials her cell phone.

"Gerry, hi. Look, my brother is…What? Oh, my God, Gerry, I…I'm so sorry. Yes. Of course."

Her face falls.

FRANCINE MAHONEY

If the Irish do death well, then Irish Catholics do death the best. And when the beloved mother of an Irish Catholic police officer dies, then it's an all-out parade of grief, drink, song and stories. Family pour in from all over with garment bags and 30 packs of beer and proceed to get so drunk that they forget who the hell even died in the first place. The relatives and friends of Francine Mahoney's are no exception as they stand graveside by her coffin, each looking more hungover than the next.

Theresa is there to represent, alongside Richie and Fiona. Her eyes meet Gerry's and hold a moment as the bagpipes begin to play Danny Boy, the Irish equivalent of a cemetery National Anthem. Theresa thinks to herself, Mom was right, this is way too sad and definitely too Irish. When the song ends (finally), Gerry gives her a sad nod and climbs into the limo. The crowd begins to disperse. Richie leans to his sister.

"Well, he finally got his limo ride."

Fiona puts an arm around Theresa. "You talk to him yet?"

"No. Not yet."

"He'll come around," she says reassuringly. "He just needs time. I mean, he just lost his mother."

"So did we," replies Theresa, the words hanging out there as if they all realize that for the first time.

They slowly walk to her car. "Well, apparently this is how you're supposed to do a funeral," says Richie.

"Kind of boring if you ask me," notes Theresa.

Fiona doesn't miss a beat. "At least we got gift bags at ours."

They stop and give their sister a 'Hey, that was pretty funny!' look. Fiona usually isn't the sarcastic one, and even she cracks a smile.

"We really are a 'chit-chow'," says Richie.

As they open the creaky doors to Theresa's Chevy Malibu and pile in, she asks, "You guys wanna hit 'the beach?'"

****

'The beach' is a gravelly strip of sand along the Shore Road parkway with a stunning view of the Verrazano Bridge, on the southernmost point of Brooklyn. The skyline of lower Manhattan looms in the distance.

The Fitzgerald kids lean against the beat-up Malibu, all still handsomely dressed in their black outfits from the service. Music plays on the car radio. Empty cans of Budweiser are strewn across the hood. They would hit the beach all the time when they were teenagers in high school. They'd buy beer with fake IDs, grab a date and check out the late-night view of Manhattan. If you couldn't get laid at 'the beach', you couldn't get laid.

"So, we gonna do this ashes thing?" asks Richie. For the first time he looks relaxed. His tie is undone. His shirttail is out - looking more like a Fitzy, that a Richard Fitzgerald.

"I haven't even opened the envelope," says Theresa, a bit tipsy.

"It's all numbers," he says. "I have no idea what they mean."

"Corey told me they're coordinates," says Fiona. "Latitude and longitude." Richie and Theresa look at each other, confused and suspicious.

"Eduardo says we have to do it, or we'll all be cursed," says Richie. "He calls it *la maldición*."

"Well, my life couldn't get much shittier right now," states Theresa as she downs another beer, making it a quick five for her. Fiona looks up at the looming Verrazano Bridge.

"I don't know what I'm so afraid of. I mean, it's not that big."

Richie and Theresa look up as well, and say in unison, "That's a big fucking bridge." They all laugh.

In the background, the song SUMMERWIND by Frank Sinatra begins to play on the car stereo and waft through the air.

The summer wind came blowin' in from across the sea
It lingered there, to touch your hair and walk with me

Fiona closes her eyes and smiles.

"Mom loved this song."

"Sinatra's the only Italian she ever tolerated," laughs Richie.

"Tolerant," snaps Theresa. "Now, there's a word never used in a sentence with her before." She's getting drunk. And pissy.

"Stop," says Fiona and takes her brother by the hand.

"Come on, Richie. Dance with me."

Theresa watches them slow dance, content and comfortable there with Fiona resting her head on her brother's shoulder. Those two were always close, and she still harbors a bit of jealousy.

"I'm going to miss her," says a swaying Fiona.

"Really?" snips Theresa. "What are you gonna miss most? The guilt? The racism? The homophobia?"

Fiona lifts her head. "Why are you so angry? And mean? Like really, really mean. God, you're getting to be just like her."

The moods are shifting.

"You know what?" says a drunk and now angry Theresa. "Fuck it. Fuck the bags. Fuck Gerry. And fuck that Bridge!" She yells the last part towards the Verrazano - but it's really aimed at her mother.

Richie looks around, he doesn't need any more trouble or bad publicity right now.

"Quiet down, will you."

"Why do you hate her so much?" Fiona asks her sister.

Theresa pushes off the hood and approaches Fiona, grabbing her wrist and staring at the rubber band.

"I hate what she did to you. What she's still doing to you. To all of us."

Richie tries to step in as the peacemaker, a completely foreign position to him. "Theresa. That's enough."

"No, Richie, it's not enough."

She turns to face Fiona. "I hated her. I hated her sharp tongue and her biting remarks. How she could cut you in half with one comment. My weight. Your hair. Richie's clothes."

She stops herself and thinks - this is it, this is the moment she lets it all out.

"Her son is being wheeled out on a stretcher, and all Mom cared about was what the fucking neighbors might think."

Fiona screams. "Stop! Stop it!"

She steps back and places her hands on her ears. Once again, she can hear her heartbeat throbbing in her ears. She closes her eyes and she's a teenager. It's 1998, and she's standing outside the Fitzgerald house. Ambulance lights flash. Neighbors are watching. Bridget Fitzgerald is standing at attention, her face full of fury and embarrassment as a stretcher is wheeled out the front door. Teenage Theresa and Fiona watch terrified as their brother Richie is carried into the ambulance, his wrist bloodied and wrapped in gauze. Bridget looks to the child beside her and begins to scream — at Fiona. It was Fiona, the baby, the softest and easiest, on the receiving end of her fury.

"What did you do? What did you do?" The words echo in Fiona's ears. She opens her eyes and she's back at 'the beach' with her brother and sister.

Theresa states softly but with purpose. "Mom would never blame herself for what Richie did. And she knew she couldn't pull that shit with me - so she dumped all the guilt on you."

Fiona's eyes well with tears. She turns to her brother.

"I should have known. We were so close. I...I should have known you were so unhappy."

"Nobody knew, Fi," says Richie. "I was scared. Stupid. I should have talked to somebody. I should have talked to you."

Theresa is calmer, more in control. "You're right, I'm angry. I'm angry because I should have stood up to her. I should have said something. I should have done more to protect you. Both of you."

She turns away, trying to hide the tears that are filling her eyes, the tough exterior melting before them. And in that moment, she realizes she has come unmoored.

Fiona walks over and holds her sister tight, tighter than ever, and whispers, "I love you."

Theresa still can't say it. She used that part of her to say it to Gerry and look where it got her. Fiona knows that. And it's OK.

They hold the embrace, and it seems like all their anger and resentment melts away. Frank Sinatra stops singing, and the random playlist on the car stereo cues up a new song.

The sisters pull back from their embrace and look at each other.

Everybody, rock your body

Mouths open. Eyes wide. Theresa exclaims, "Oh. My. God."

Everybody, rock your body right

"I love this song!" says Fiona, about to bust.

Backstreet's back, alright!

The Backstreet Boys song blares on the stereo as the girls start to sing at the top of their lungs and dance like teenagers.

Richie puts up with it for a few minutes, then reaches into the car. Click. The music stops.

"Awe. You're no fun, *Richard!*" says Theresa, mocking him.

"No way. I had to listen to that shit every morning before school."

The girls crack up.

Fiona gets an idea. "Hey, let's shotgun a beer."

"Definitely," agrees Theresa enthusiastically.

"Are you kidding? It's bad enough I'm drinking this stuff, now you want me to drink it fast?" says Richie.

"Come on, Richard," coaxes Fiona, and grabs a can of beer for each of them.

"How do you even do this?" she asks, fumbling with the car keys.

"Careful, you two," says Richie vigorously wiping the top of his clean. "This is a three-thousand-dollar suit."

Theresa puts a hand on Richard's shoulder, looking like she's about to give impactful words of wisdom. "I'm gonna give you some great advice that I got the other day. Stop being such a dickhead."

Jesus, he thinks, I really am a pretentious prick.

Theresa grabs the cans and keys.

"Ok. Ready? You pop the top and drink it here, from this hole. Go!"

KSSSHH! They each shotgun a beer. Fiona slams hers to the ground and pumps her arms in victory. "Yeah! Woo Hoo! Fuck that bridge!"

Theresa smiles at her sister, sure that the outburst was meant for the Verrazano and not their mother.

They are all beyond happy. Smiling. Drunk. Having the time of their lives. Wait. Something is wrong. Richie and Theresa look at Fiona.

"Fiona? Sweetie? You OK?"

Fiona's face contorts. Her ears throb and ring, only this time, it's not a flashback…it's…it's…BLAAAAP! Projectile vomit spews out her mouth and all over Richie's three-thousand-dollar suit. Manhattan's top fashion designer is covered in beer and puke.

Theresa deadpans, "Ooh, too bad that's not a 'Buy One, Get One'."

FITZGERALD HOUSE

Fiona shuffles in slowly, nursing her head from yesterday's beer guzzling adventures. She must be hungover because she pours herself a huge cup of black coffee, not herbal tea. In fact, she looks exactly like Theresa sitting there slumped over her mug.

Richard timidly enters the kitchen, his Manhattan swagger lost along with his puke-stained suit and shoes. He looks like he just stepped out of the 90s, wearing baggy stone washed jeans, Skechers sneakers, an oversized neon t-shirt, and a sports jacket with padded shoulders. Fiona looks up wearily from her mug.

"Am I still drunk, or did we go back in time?"

Richie says nothing and pours himself an equal sized mug of black coffee.

"I'm sorry about the suit," says Fiona. "Send me the dry cleaning bill."

Richie takes a sip. Ugh, this is awful. The hits just keep on coming.

"Forget it. I'm just gonna burn it. They say fashion is retro, but I honestly hope I never see this look again."

He leans against the counter and scans his 'totally heinous' outfit.

"I've seen that look before," says Fiona.

"I know. In 1998."

"No, not the clothes. I mean, you're getting an idea, aren't you?"

"I think so," says Richie with a smirk, his wheels turning.

****

Theresa is in the living room on a Yoga mat meditating. Headband. Sweat suit. Listening to John Tesh music and trying to embrace her inner Chi by looking for cows in parking lots. Maybe Fiona *does* know something. A knock at the front door breaks her trance. She looks out the window and sees Gerry. Holy shit! He can't see her like this.

She slams the music to stop and rips off the headband. Breathing heavy, she opens the door and tries to act casual.

"Gerry. Hey. How's it...how you doin'?"

"Good morning, Theresa. Sorry to bother you. Is you father home?" asks Gerry. He's all business in his New York Police Department uniform.

"My father? Sure. He's, ah, he's not out on the porch?"

She yells upstairs. "Dad?"

Fiona and Richard enter from the kitchen.

"Hey Gerry," says Fiona as she gives him a big, loving hug.

"We're all so sorry about your Mom."

"Thanks, Fi. And thanks for coming to the service. Sorry I didn't get a chance to talk to you guys."

Silence. They're all uncomfortable.

Gerry scans Richard's outfit up and down (the way Richard has done to Tilton and other people thousands of times) then turns to Theresa.

"Why is Richie dressed like Chandler Bing?"

Michaleen descends the stairs. "Gerry! Grand, grand. I'll throw on the sausage."

"No, Mr. Fitzgerald. Thank you."

"*Mister* Fitzgerald? Aren't we official. And don't you look dapper in your outfit."

"It's a uniform," says Gerry with extraordinary pride.

"What's this all about, then?" asks Michaleen.

Gerry turns and opens the door. In walks Mrs. Flanagan. Theresa is pissed. The one morning she spends trying yoga and bullshit mediation is immediately lost. "What the hell does she want?"

"Theresa, please. Mrs. Flanagan, could you repeat the statement you gave earlier?" asks Officer Mahoney of the NYPD. (He's secretly loving all this formality.)

"I will indeed," states Rose Flanagan. She loves to be the one to provide any and all information. "I was walking Topper, like I do every morn' at half six. Well, there's been a lot of unusual activity around here lately."

She doesn't say so much as spit each observation in the direction of her intended target.

First Michaleen.

"Men sleepin' outside."

Then Richard.

"Flashy sports cars racing up and down the street."

Finally, she looks at Theresa with disgust.

"And obscene profanity," she blesses herself and continues with her revelations. "Well, like I said, I was takin' Topper to do his business, and mindin' my own like I always do..."

The Fitzgerald family gives exasperated eye rolls in sync. Even Gerry has a tough time buying that one.

"I happen to look up to the porch, and sittin' there is Michaleen Fitzgerald himself. I figgered he was sleepin' out there again. Can you imagine, Officer? Sleepin' on a stoop. Have you heard of such a thing? Maybe I shouldn't say anymore. I like to mind to my own knitting."

More eye rolls. Gerry, doing his best to be patient and kind, asks her to please continue.

"Well, I notice he's up to something. So, I go up me driveway to get a better view, and there I see it. Mixin' and pourin', like. Powder, it is. And he's placin' it into plastic bags."

Michaleen bursts, "What'r ye goin' on about, woman?!"

"I watch NCIS," she states. "I know what the powder and the bags mean."

"That was Bridget, ye feckin' eejit!" spits Michaleen

"Bridget?! Don't you blaspheme that poor woman, not even here to defend herself. The years she put up with you and your philanderin'." She looks at Gerry. "The women he's had."

"Awe, you wish," shoots Michaleen.

This is it, he thinks to himself. This just might just be the day Michaleen breaks a Ninth Commandment and actually kills someone.

Rose crosses her arm, "Well, I never…"

Michaleen points a thumb at Theresa. "See. I told ye!"

He turns to Gerry, "Are ye gonna listen to this crazy old lesbian?! Her and that masturbatin' dog she's got there."

Gerry tries to regain control. "Alright. Everybody settle down."

Mrs. Flanagan is full of accusation. "It's all there in his backpack, Officer. Go on, check for yourself."

"Mr. Fitzgerald," says Gerry as kindly as he can. "I'll need to see the bag."

Michaleen doesn't budge. "Not me Go bag. No way."

Theresa steps in. "Give him the bag, Dad."

A tense standoff. This could go either way.

Fiona speaks up, "Daddy? Give him the bag."

Nope. Mick holds on tight. Richie's face is full of disgust. I knew it. My own father, he thinks, a drug dealer. Christ, the press will have a field day with this one.

Theresa grabs the backpack from her father. "Just give it to him, already."

As she wrestles it away, the backpack bursts open and bags hit the floor. Reds. Greens. Yellows.

Mrs. Flanagan is puffed with confidence, "See. Just like I told ye."

Fiona is aghast, staring at the scattered bags strewn about. "Is...is that Mom?!"

"No, it's not yer mother," says Mick.

"It's cocaine, isn't it?" Richard looks to Theresa. "See, I told you."

"Don't be daft," spits Michaleen. "It's not cocaine. It's...it's..."

Gerry, bent down inspecting the contents, proclaims his discovery with the confidence of someone who has just solved New York city's toughest crime.

"It's cannabis."

"Wait. What?" exclaims Theresa.

Officer Gerald Mahoney, NYPD, confirms. "Marijauna. Weed."

All eyes are on Michaleen. He waves a hand. "Everyone just relax. It's all legal, like." He pulls his wallet out and hands a paper to Gerry.

"Sure, now he has his wallet," mutters Richie. Gerry gives him a nod that says, "I know, right."

"For medicinal purposes only," declares Michaleen. "Have yiz been to Florida? State's full of nursing homes and rehabs. Feckin' depressing. The whole place is like God's waiting room."

"Why are they all in colored bags?" asks Fiona.

"Helps me keep track of the customers." Michaleen points to each baggie in colored succession. "Red's cataracts. Green's dementia. Yellow's hip replacement."

Gerry regains control. "Your father's working for a Marijuana Treatment Center," he says handing the license back to Michaleen. "By New York law, anything over 25 grams is a misdemeanor. That means a hefty fine and a potential jail sentence."

There's a moment where all fear the stern-by-the-book Officer Mahoney might actually arrest their father. But good old Gerry from the neighborhood relents.

"These look to be under the legal limit. But driving it across state lines will make it a punishable offence."

"I'm not *driving* it anywhere," replies Michaleen with a sheepish grin. He knows that one of the benefits of being sixty-seven and without obligations is that you're rarely required to explain yourself.

"Well, I'm sorry to bother you all," says Gerry.

He escorts Mrs. Flanagan out and turns back to look at Theresa. They share a moment - it's obvious he still cares for her, and she misses him.

Theresa closes the door with a hint of sadness and says, "We gotta get rid of those fuckin' ashes."

BROOKLYN HOSPITAL

For as much as she may hate the grinding traffic light commute, Theresa loves working at the hospital - her tough exterior and biting sarcasm mask her huge, caring heart. Other people might crumble in the situations she's been in. Holding a mother as her teenage son is prepped for surgery from a bullet wound. Comforting a family after the doctor has delivered terminal news. Rubbing the back of a pregnant teenager writhing in pain from the onset of labor. Fiona can have her art and poetry. Richie can have his glamorous Manhattan lifestyle. Theresa is perfectly content and ideally suited to be an emergency room nurse. This is the job she was born for.

Theresa walks through the admitting area, past Shelagh.

"No pissy remark this morning? You're losing your edge, Red."

Shelagh stands to meet her.

"Theresa. Listen, I need to…" says Shelagh nervously. "There's a patient in room seven. She didn't want me to tell you, but…"

"Who? Abby again? I told that kid no soccer games."

"No. It's not Abby."

Theresa looks at her cousin. Something's not right.

****

Fiona lies in a hospital bed looking pale – paler than usual. She tries not to cry when her big sister pulls back the curtain and enters the room.

"I..I don't know what happened. I thought the cramps might have been from my morning yoga stretches, but they grew more intense."

"Do you want me to call Corey?" asks Nurse Theresa.

"No. Don't call him. He's at school. I didn't want him to know yet. Not until I was certain."

"Certain of what?" asks Theresa.

Fiona waits on the answer for a few seconds, and looks to her belly. "We've been trying for a while."

"But, you're not..." says Theresa, a bit taken aback.

"What, married? You mean, like, in a church? You're not serious, are you? Corey says all religion is based on fear, smoke, and murder."

"Jesus, he sounds like Dad," says Theresa.

Fiona decided to leave all that pay, pray and obey stuff a long time ago. Too many of the prayers were just words to her that never stuck. She found her spiritual guidance in yoga, Buddhism, art and poetry - that's how

Fiona nourished her soul. Take away the rolled-up floor mat and the incense, she was pretty much on an even keel with Michaleen in her disdain for all things Catholic.

"I'm not looking for your permission, Theresa. And I certainly don't need your judgement."

She suddenly feels a sharp pain in her side. It's getting worse, and more intense. The nurse in Theresa rushes into action and the sister in her takes Fiona's hand.

"I'm sorry, Fi. Close your eyes. Breath. Think about the cow in the parking lot."

Fiona laughs through the pain.

"Fuck you."

Theresa softens. "It's probably just an ovarian cyst, but we want to make sure," her tone reassuring her scared little sister.

"So, I'm gonna be an Auntie, huh?"

"Would be pretty cool, right?" says Fiona, the realization that she may be pregnant starting to sink in. "I hope I'll be a good mother."

"You will be," says Theresa tenderly.

Fiona takes her sister's hands and together they lay them on the new born life growing inside her belly. It will be different, having a child and a family. Fiona wouldn't be cold and distant like her own mother. Whatever their child wanted to become, Fiona would support them lovingly, carefully, wholeheartedly. It will be the beginning of a new Fitzgerald generation. The bitterness ends.

Theresa squeezes her hand. "You're gonna be OK." Fiona looks at her big sister with a confident, caring smile. "We all are."

The curtain track slide open. "Gerry?" says a surprised Theresa. "What are you doing here? Is everyone OK?"

Gerry looks like he ran all the way to the hospital.

"Yes. Well, no. Yes. You OK, Fiona? Shelagh called me."

Fiona smiles, radiating calmness as she rubs her belly. "I'm fine, Gerry. Thanks."

"It's not my father, is it?" asks a ruffled Theresa.

"No. I really need to speak with you," he replies.

"Not now."

"But I gotta tell you something."

"I'm with a patient," says Theresa curtly. Knowing everyone's OK, she turns from surprised to pissed. Gerry takes a deep breath and delivers his news as if he's practiced this speech for days.

"I've decided that I like the view. And, yes."

"You like the...Yes, what?"

"Yes to your question."

"Yes about my father? He's not OK?"

"No. I mean, yes, he's OK. Jeeze, you're right, this isn't easy. Just listen for a minute, will ya? I like the view. I like the view from your couch watching John Wayne movies. I like the view from your porch, watching you sidestep around Topper's dog poop. I like the view from the passenger seat, watching you get all steamed, waiting for red lights to change."

Theresa is softening. Fiona smiles at them both.

"Now, don't get me wrong," says Gerry. "You did an OK job. I mean, for your first proposal and all. But, I realized I was doing it all wrong. You really do need flowers and music."

He turns, and Shelagh appears from behind the curtains holding a boom box stereo. She hits play and Elvis Presley begins to croon.

Wise men say, Only fools rush in

But I can't help falling in love with you.

Shall I stay? Would it be a sin

If I can't help falling in love with you?

Gerry gets down on one knee. Theresa's hands cover her mouth. He reaches back and pulls a ring box from his pocket.

"Theresa Kathleen Genevieve Fitzgerald. For the fourth, and final time - will you marry me?"

Theresa looks to Fiona. Then to Shelagh. Then back to Gerry.

She stands, surveying the situation, not sure where to go from here. She thinks. And waits. It seems like an eternity.

BROOKLYN

A room is filled with rolls of cloth and long cutting tables. The sound of sewing machines grind in the background. This is where the magic happens, where the designs of Richard Fitzgerald are born and take shape. Richard rarely comes out here, he's more the idea behind the creation, not the physical creation itself.

When he first started out, he did everything. Cut fabric. Carried heavy woolen rolls of cloth. Laid out patterns on tables. God forbid a teenage boy from Brooklyn ever declare his desire to be a seamstress. Sew? Clothes? Fashion? Richard hid all that in the dark confines of his teenage mind. It was bad enough when he told his mother he didn't want to play sports.

For all his Gameslayer, ladies' man, outlaw, Golden Globes boxer bravado, Michaleen was surprisingly supportive of his son. He never once made Richard feel uncomfortable or ashamed of his lifestyle choices. The Rose Flanagans of the world would whisper in hushed tones and there would be muffled conversations at Kelly's, but no one was ever foolish enough to say anything directly to Michaleen about his son.

Tilton enters the factory floor and is immediately surprised to see Richard standing there, as if he was waiting for him.

"Richard. I...I didn't expect you. I brought the sketches, just like you asked me to. These designs are very..." he searches for the right word."They're very retro."

"I'm trying something new. And my car keys?"

"Yes. Of course. Not a scratch."

Richard walks slowly, his hand brushing against the bright patterned rolls of wool and cashmere and silk. "You know, Tilton, this is a tough business."

"Yes, Richard. I know. Very tough."

"It's an industry filled with copy cats and knockoffs. But, I really think you could make it."

Tilton smiles proudly. Richard steps in close, scanning Tilton's outfit up and down.

"You have passion, and drive. And you certainly have imagination."

"Thank you, Richard."

"I hired you because of your impressive background. Parsons School of Fashion. Top ten percent of your class."

Tilton is beaming.

"You must have worked very hard. In fact, you probably would have finished in the top five percent of your class...if you didn't get caught."

Tilton's smile fades.

"I did some digging with HR. Seems you love to take things that don't belong to you. Test scores. Homework assignments. Designs. Surnames."

Tilton's mouth is dry. He begins to sweat on his upper lip. Richard is toying with him like a cat plays with a mouse before the kill, flipping it between its paws, barely letting it escape before chomping down for the kill.

"Hedge funds and houses on Martha's Vineyard? Seriously? I don't have a problem that you made up a family. I think it shows creativity. The problem I do have is, you're always trying to be somebody else. Whether it's some made up name like 'Tilton Masters'. Or Richard Fitzgerald. Or Marco Pacelli."

Richard begins to adjust at Tilton's outfit, pulling at a sleeve, brushing off the scarf, undoing the double-buttoned jacket. (Does this kid ever listen? One button, he told him. Always one button.)

"It all lacks a certain amount of originality. I mean, I can see how it might be embarrassing to tell people your family fortune came from pumping septic tanks all over Massapequa, Long Island. Isn't that right? Isn't your real name Timothy Mastrangelo?"

Richie snaps his fingers trying to recall something, "What's the slogan again? The numbers?"

Tilton is far too embarassed to say it aloud, and mumbles something.

"I'm sorry. What? What was that?"

Tilton is dying inside, and slowly states the Mastrangleo Septic Service Trucks Slogan, "Your number two is our number one."

Richard stifles a laugh. "Right. You see, *Timmy*, where you're from is as important as who you're from. You should never hide from your family."

He looks Tilton in the eye, squares his shoulders and states proudly, "My Grandfather was a fisherman from Galway. My father climbed telephone poles. I'm really just a tailor from Bay Ridge, New York. And you?" he says as nonchalant and emotionless as sending back a bottle of wine, "You're fired."

Tilton's shoulders drop.

"Oh, and one other thing...." Richard looks beyond Tilton to a police officer standing beside the exit. He's holding a small green baggie filled with cocaine.

"You're under arrest."

Richard watches as the officer handcuffs Tilton and leads him away, then mutters, "We gotta get rid of those fuckin' ashes."

BROOKLYN * MANHATTAN * LONG ISLAND

The first hint of light peers over New York. Instructions in hand, the Fitzgerald children each set out to fulfill their mothers final wish and rid themselves of the ashes, and the curse. *La maldición.*

Theresa sits at a traffic light, the plastic red baggie on her lap. She's different this time - calm, relaxed, almost....Zen. The light turns green, but she doesn't notice it or move. Her eyes are too busy looking down at the engagement ring sparkling on her finger. She smiles wide. Actually, she's beaming.

A horn blasts behind her - BEEEEP! She looks up to the rear-view mirror.

"Shaddup!"

So much for Zen. This patience thing may take some time. She puts the car in gear and proceeds cautiously, but happily through the intersection.

****

Fiona sits on a park bench, staring at the sea, a soft wind brushes across the calm look of determination on her face.

The yellow baggie lays on her lap, against her stomach and the new life awaiting inside her.

****

Richard drives his Porsche slowly down a quiet Manhattan side street, wet and dark and full of reflections. He looks at the green baggie on the passenger seat beside him. It sits atop a fashion magazine with a headline that reads:

MARCO PACELLI 1990s INSPIRED COLLECTION A MAJOR FLOP! Could it <u>BE</u> more heinous?

He smiles - payback's a bitch - and continues to drive, searching for his note card destination.

****

Cell phones ring as the siblings conference each other in from their locations.

"Everybody there?" asks Richie.

"I'm here," says Fiona

"Theresa?" asks Richie.

"Yep," she says into her speaker phone "Where are you guys?"

"I'm in the East Village," says Richie, his head twisting left and right to see where he's going.

"I'm at Fort Hamilton," says Fiona.

"Wait, is Corey with you?" asks Richie. "We're supposed to do this alone."

Fiona responds proudly, "Nope. I drove over the bridge all by myself."

Her brother and sister beam with pride.

"Way to go, Fi," says Theresa.

"Good for you, kid," says Richie. "Theresa, where are you?"

Theresa drives slowly through a congested area of strip malls and gas stations, totally lost and confused. She looks at her note card: **Theresa 40.655509 -73.604247**

"I have no idea. This is really stupid."

"Come on," says Richie. "We said we'd do this. Hold on. I think I found mine."

The Porsche stops. Richard gets out and walks to a large cast iron gate, nearly stepping on a homeless man propped against the opening.

A sign reads: "**THE CREATIVE LITTLE GARDEN. A community backyard maintained by volunteers from the neighborhood.**"

The gate swings open and Richard walks into a lavish green garden of ferns, flowers and plants.

Fiona's voice comes through his phone. "You good Richie? Richie?"

Mesmerized, he slowly enters an oasis of tranquility.

"Yeah. Yeah, I'm good."

****

Theresa is still driving, starting to get pissed. "This is so stupid. Wait. This can't be right." She looks at the directions in her hand.

"Theresa. Where are you?" asks Fiona.

Theresa looks up. "PepBoys. I'm at a fucking PepBoys on Long Island."

"You sure you have the right coordinates?" asks Fiona.

They can both hear Richard laughing on his end of the phone. "Maybe Mom thought you needed a fan belt or something."

"Well, at least she got my color right," says Theresa. "I'm really pissed now."

Theresa's car pulls into the empty parking lot. "Is this your idea of a joke Fiona? Because if I step in some Buddhist cow shit, I'm gonna kill somebody."

"What is she talking about?" asks Richard.

"Nothing," says Fiona. "Where are you exactly? Text me your address."

"Baldwin, Long Island. Here, I'll send it to you."

Theresa sends the text. The creaky door to her Chevy Malibu opens and she steps out to look around. Slowly, her face changes. Something seems familiar. She whispers softly, "Holy shit."

Fiona's voice is heard through the phone. "Theresa? You there?"

But Theresa isn't listening. She's lost as realization washes over her.

"I know where I am," she says. "Nunley's. This place used to be Nunley's Amusement Park."

"Mom never took us there," says Richie.

"Yes. She did," says Theresa as it begins to sink in. "We used to come here before you two were born."

Fiona has looked up information and reads aloud.

"Nunley's Happyland Amusement Park. Built in Brooklyn 1912. Moved to Long Island in the 1940's to make way for the Belt Parkway. It closed when PepBoys bought the land in 1990."

Theresa is surprised by her own emotion and intensity as a flood of memories cascade over her. She looks around with wonder. "There was a Ferris wheel. Bumper Boats. A little roller coaster.   Mom and I would ride the Murphy Carousel right there. That was her favorite."

And tears form. Real tears. Fitzgeralds, so famously known for not doing sad, do in fact cry. "I think it was the only time I remember Mom being happy. Like, really happy."

And then Theresa realizes something about her mother, something she hadn't thought about or refused to believe or even see. Bridget Fitzgerald gave her family all she had, the only way she knew how, and if that wasn't enough, so be it. A cheating husband. A drunk, cold father. Maybe she might have been different if her life was different. By the time Theresa finally noticed or even cared, her mother was gone. She looks at the plastic red baggie in her hand and speaks to her brother and sister with determination and resolve.

"Let's do this."

They each peel back their colored plastic bag and release their mother's ashes.

Theresa's waft across the parking lot.

Richard's fall among the green plants and ferns.

Fiona's blow into the sea below the Verrazano Bridge.

As the bags empty, they each find a curled note taped to the inside.   The flowing, cursive handwriting is familiar. Bridget Fitzgerald speaks directly to each of her children.

"If the bag is empty, then you found your note and you fulfilled my wishes. I know what you're thinking – the colors and all. But you're wrong."

"My beautiful, agitated Theresa. I'm sure you think your bag is red for anger. It's not. It's for love - love that you sometimes can't see, or even hear...you just need to know where to look for it, because it can be in the strangest places. But it's there. It always was."

Richard sits, surrounded by the lavish greenery and reads his mother's note.

"Richard. You surround yourself with material things. Clothes. Cars. Money. That's not what's important, son - and in the end, it'll just leave you hollow and empty. Look around. See the beauty of nature. That's the only green that really matters. It's a rare combination, someone who has a love of life and a firm understanding of what's important – the simplicity of living a life with those you love. And when you've found that kind of peace, then you'll know what it is to be truly happy."

Fiona reads her note on the bench at Fort Hamilton, just below the sprawling Verrazano Bridge.

"My baby girl, Fiona. It must be exhausting being you - knowing you can't turn your brain off. I'm sure there are times when all

you want to do is run and hide away from it all - but you don't. You get up and you face the world every day. I sent you to a fortress that's been the home to brave soldiers for over 100 years, because you're the bravest person I know. Yellow is not for fear or anxiety, it's the color of sunshine, and hope, and happiness. And that's what I wish for all three of you."

They can see that the final paragraph of the note is written by their father, in his choppy hard-pressed penmanship. For two people who seemingly hated each other, Michaleen and Bridget finally found something they could do together.

"Now, I'm sure I'll die soon enough from stubbornness and whiskey - but until then, I plan to grab life by the lapels, give it a kiss, and swing it back out onto the dance floor. I suggest yiz all do the same."

They each smile and take in the moment.

Theresa's memories.

Fiona's courage.

Richard's tranquility.

As he exits the garden, Richard unclasps the watch from his wrist and rubs a thumb over faint scars left from a regrettable act of teenage confusion and frustration.

He places the watch - the Patek Phillipe - alongside the homeless man, then smiles and mutters to himself, "timeless."

****

Traditional Irish music plays as Michaleen plops his hands on his knees and stands for one last ritual, checking his front pocket, back pocket, lips for his keys, wallet and teeth.

He puts an arm around Caitlin as they cruise along New York harbor in her yacht and watch a glorious sun rise over Manhattan, covering the landscape in reds, yellows and greens.

The final sentence of the note to his children rings in his head.

"And get out on deck every once in a while. The view is so much better on deck."

ACKNOWLEDGEMENT

While scanning the Boston Globe back in December of 2016, I came across a 'death notice for the ages.' This obituary for Chris Connors of York, Maine, written by his daughter Caitlin and her cousin Liz served as my inspiration for the essence of Michaleen - along with the great Irish actor Barry Fitzgerald of THE QUIET MAN and GOING MY WAY films.

The Irish know how to live, so they know how to die.

Irishman Dies from Stubbornness, Whiskey

Chris Connors died, at age 67, after trying to box his bikini-clad hospice nurse just moments earlier. Ladies man, game slayer, and outlaw Connors told his last inappropriate joke on Friday, December 9, 2016, that which cannot be printed here. Anyone else fighting ALS and stage 4 pancreatic cancer would have gone quietly into the night, but Connors was stark naked drinking Veuve in a house full of friends and family as Al Green played from the speakers. The way he died is just like he lived: he wrote his own rules, he fought authority and he paved his own way. And if you said he couldn't do it, he would make sure he could.

Most people thought he was crazy for swimming in the ocean in January; for being a skinny Irish Golden Gloves boxer from

Quincy, Massachusetts; for dressing up as a priest and then proceeding to get into a fight at a Jewish deli. Many gawked at his start of a career on Wall Street without a financial background - but instead with an intelligent, impish smile, love for the spoken word, irreverent sense of humor, and stunning blue eyes that could make anyone fall in love with him.

As much as people knew hanging out with him would end in a night in jail or a killer screwdriver hangover, he was the type of man that people would drive 16 hours at the drop of a dime to come see. He lived 1000 years in the 67 calendar years we had with him because he attacked life; he grabbed it by the lapels, kissed it, and swung it back onto the dance floor. At the age of 26 he planned to circumnavigate the world - instead, he ended up spending 40 hours on a life raft off the coast of Panama. In 1974, he founded the Quincy Rugby Club. In his thirties, he sustained a knife wound after saving a woman from being mugged in New York City. He didn't slow down: at age 64, he climbed to the base camp of Mount Everest. Throughout his life, he was an accomplished hunter and birth control device tester (with some failures, notably Caitlin Connors, 33; Chris Connors, 11; and Liam Connors, 8).

He was a rare combination of someone who had a love of life and a firm understanding of what was important - the simplicity of living a life with those you love. Although he threw some of the most memorable parties during the greater half of a century, he would trade it all for a night in front of the fire with his family in Maine. His acute awareness of the importance of a life lived with the ones you love over any material possession was only handicapped by his territorial attachment to the remote control of his Sonos music.

Chris enjoyed cross dressing, a well-made fire, and mashed potatoes with lots of butter. His regrets were few, but include eating a rotisserie hot dog from an unmemorable convenience store in the summer of 1986.

Of all the people he touched, both willing and unwilling, his most proud achievement in life was marrying his wife Emily Ayer Connors who supported him in all his glory during his heyday, and lovingly supported him physically during their last days together.

Absolut vodka and Simply Orange companies are devastated by the loss of Connors. A "Celebration of Life" will be held during Happy Hour (4 p.m.) at York Harbor Inn on Monday, December 19.

In lieu of flowers, please pay open bar tab or donate to Connors' water safety fund at www.thechrisconnorsfund.com.

*Reprinted with permission from Caitlin Connors

ABOUT THE AUTHOR

Mike Bernard is a founding partner of The ChathamPoint Group, an executive search firm outside Boston, MA. His 'midlife crisis' writing career began when his children and his money went off to college - checks made out to Loyola University Maryland (x2) and Assumption College respectively. Mike's work has placed in the NICHOLL FELLOWSHIP, BLUECAT, and FINAL DRAFT Big Break Screenplay contests, and was a TOP 10 FINALIST in the PAGE International screenplay competition. Three of his screenplays were optioned and under development with production companies. A FISHERMAN'S VIEW is his first novel.

Mike is a graduate of Providence College and Boston College High School. He resides in Medfield, MA with his wife Michele.
He spends summers on the beaches of Cape Cod and winters roaming the aisles of Home Depot.

Contact: <u>Meb123@comcast.net</u>
Facebook: @AFishermansView

Made in the USA
Columbia, SC
25 October 2018